I0817687

Praise for

THE COLD HOUSE

"A wonderfully gripping modern gothic tale of haunting, grief, secrets and lies. A remote community, an unreliable narrator, and twisty reveals that keep on coming—I read it in one sitting! Highly recommended!"

SARAH PINBOROUGH, the #1 international bestselling author of *We Live Here Now* and Netflix's *Behind Her Eyes*

"*The Cold House* is a unique blend of folk and grief horror—emotionally raw, captivating, and a twisting, winding descent into darkness. No one does it like Slatter. I'm a fan for life!"

SADIE HARTMANN 'Mother Horror', Bram Stoker Award®-winning author of *101 Horror Books to Read Before You're Murdered*

"Old magic and fresh grief twist together, weaving a growing dread that builds to an explosive conclusion."

KELLEY ARMSTRONG, #1 bestselling author of the Rip Through Time series and *Every Step She Takes*

"Claustrophobic and elegantly plotted, *The Cold House* is full of grief, mystery, and the pain of family secrets. Slatter just keeps getting better!"

CHRISTOPHER GOLDEN, *New York Times* bestselling author of *The Night Birds* and *The House of Last Resort*

"A luscious little labyrinth of a book, drenched in ambiance and dripping with delicious prose, full of twists, turns, terror, torment, and triumph."

DELILAH S. DAWSON, *New York Times* bestselling author of *Bloom* and *Guillotine*

"A gorgeous and unsettling entry into the horror genre. Slatter melds grief and folk horror with a master's touch. There's a tender brutality in her turns of phrase and a humanity in her characters that will move even the hardest soul. If I dared, I'd beg a final request to keep reading and reading and reading."

Kristi DeMeester, author of
Dark Sisters and *Such a Pretty Smile*

"A masterclass in storytelling. Slatter rolls out her devastating revelations smoothly and with perfect timing, drawing us into this sad, terrifying novella with ease, and chilling us to the bone."

Kaaron Warren, author of *The Underhistory*

"Starting with the classic set up to a psychological thriller, *The Cold House* quickly morphs into something darker and stranger. Reminiscent of folk horror classics *The Wicker Man* and *Robin Redbreast*, this slice of rural noir is punchy, pacy and atmospheric."

Olivia Isaac-Henry author of
The Verdict and *Sorrow Spring*

THE COLD HOUSE

ALSO BY A.G. SLATTER
AND AVAILABLE FROM TITAN BOOKS

All the Murmuring Bones
The Path of Thorns
The Briar Book of the Dead
The Crimson Road

THE COLD HOUSE

A.G. SLATTER

TITAN BOOKS

The Cold House
Print edition ISBN: 9781835412541
E-book edition ISBN: 9781835412558

Published by Titan Books
A division of Titan Publishing Group Ltd
144 Southwark Street, London SE1 0UP
www.titanbooks.com

First edition: October 2025
10 9 8 7 6 5 4 3 2 1

A CIP catalogue record for this title is available from the British Library.

EU RP (for authorities only)
eucomply OÜ, Pärnu mnt. 139b--14, 11317 Tallinn, Estonia
hello@eucompliancepartner.com, +3375690241

Designed and typeset in ITC Berkeley Oldstyle by Richard Mason.

Printed and bound by CPI Group (UK) Ltd, Croydon, CR0 4YY.

There are Dark Ladies, and even devils bow down before them.

ST CRISPIN OF ANGLESEY,
Observations and Terrors, 1139 AD

1

'Outta the feckin way.'

I don't know how long I've been standing in front of the ice cream section of the supermarket freezer, but it's clearly long enough to piss someone off. These fugues are becoming more and more frequent, but I haven't mentioned them to anyone. It's four months *since*. Besides, who would I tell? What would be the point? It's a problem for another day, because today's is the tall, scrawny teenager next to me who can't get to the Chunky Monkey. I step aside.

'Very sorry,' I say in a tone that implies *Fuck you very much*. I'm getting good at that one, in fact it seems to be my default. A couple of feet down the aisle, I hear him mutter 'Stupid cunt'; then footsteps. Count to three, kick my foot out to the right, angle the trolley so that when he goes down he grazes his face on the shiny metal cage of its body.

'So very sorry,' I say as I leave him behind and continue shopping, an act which consists largely of tossing random things into the trolley until there looks like there might be enough to make some variety of meals if only I can focus. My jeans are hanging low, just the jut of my hip bones between me and indecency. The T-shirt, I've realised, is redolent of several days' wear, which is a nice way of saying almost-reeks-but-not-quite. It's not like I've given up on showering, but I can't recall the last time I brushed my hair. Birds will nest in it and cats will start coming to my house, meowing to get in.

I really do need to get my shit together.

It's late, almost nine, and the registers are empty of all but dull-eyed cashiers, standing around, looking stoned. Could be that, could just be life. Could be exhaustion after spending their days at uni or other jobs, their nights here trying to get enough money to keep body and soul together. The girl with shockingly red hair and equally shocking pale skin jerks to life as I thump the bottle of milk onto the conveyor belt, like a sensor light reacting to movement.

'Oh, hey,' she squeaks, and reaches for the items I'm stacking up in brisk order. The scanner bloops, sounding wet and happy at the same time, like a gum bubble bursting. I watch the stream of groceries: for the most part it looks like a five-year-old did the choosing, but there's some pasta, some meat, a few fresh vegetables, some apples and lemons. Fighting off scurvy for another week, pretending I'll cook something. The total keeps climbing and the girl – her badge says KAIT – shoots looks at me as if awaiting a complaint, a wince at least. I hold her gaze, gunfighter-style. It doesn't matter, there's more money than I can spend in a lifetime just waiting. Insurance policy, pension; payouts after the accident. Plus the money I didn't even know he had. A property portfolio, another of shares. So I spend like there's no tomorrow on food I don't generally eat – no ice cream, obviously, not today. Occasionally some booze, but who wants to be a cliché, and nowadays I don't handle hangovers well enough to take to drinking like it's a full-time job.

The last packet of crisps goes into the bags. Kait swallows hard and stammers out the total. Unblinking, I swipe the credit card like I've done every week for the past month. There's always a different cashier, it seems, or I just haven't paid attention. A distinct possibility.

'You have a good evening,' she says brightly, but I can already see her interest fading.

'Thanks, Kait. Hope you can get home soon.'

'Oh, another couple of hours.' She grins at the use of her name, interest returning.

'Then I hope you get to sleep in.'

'Early classes.'

Oh. 'Bummer.'

'Yeah.'

I push the trolley towards the automatic doors, give Kait a wave and what might pass for a smile. Maybe the most interaction I've had with a human – the ferret in the cold goods aisle notwithstanding – in months. A bright flare of contact warmth, but even now grief's sharp nails are tightening on my back, digging in, reminding me it's still there. The loss. The emptiness. The hollow inside me with that shrivelled heart rolling around – shake me like a maraca and you'd hear the rattle.

Out in the car park heat still radiates up from the tarmac, I parked close by the entrance, under the buzzing lights. It doesn't take long to load everything, haphazard, in the back of the rental. I'm in the driver's seat, sliding the key into the ignition when something hits the window beside me.

A hand, that leaves a bloody print. A face, red at the left temple, staring eyes. Not angry, but bewildered. Swaying as if there's a strong breeze or he's in a tank of water. He hits the window again and I hesitate. He reels back. I make a decision, open the door, get out. He trembles and drops to sit on the ground, head in hands and moaning, 'Why'd you do that?'

I crouch, slide two fingers under his chin, pry his hand away from the wound. 'You shouldn't have sworn at me. It's very rude. You don't know what people are going through.'

'Fuck.'

'See? You did it again. Have you learned nothing?' I can't quite figure out if his pupils are dilated from shock, concussion or the weed I can smell on him this close up. He really needed that ice cream, I guess. 'Are you dizzy?'

He nods, stops quickly.

'OK.' I rise, move behind him, put my hands under

his arms – bad choice, in the twin caves of his sweaty pits – and heave him upwards. No padding; I can feel his ribs. 'C'mon.'

'Are you abducting me, lady?'

'You should be so lucky. Hospital. Just in case.' I walk him around to the passenger's side, strap him in. 'Don't make me regret this.'

2

And I'd got home, back to the flat that doesn't feel right anymore because I'm the only one in it. And I filled the fridge and cupboard with all the things I'd bought, including the cheese and milk that sat in the car for too long while I took that idiot into A&E and waited with him the whole time. When they asked what happened, I said, 'He fell' and he didn't contradict me, because maybe he figured no one would have much sympathy for him being, quite frankly, a cunt. Or maybe he figured he might score some good painkillers for a bit. Or just maybe it was the closest thing to human kindness he'd experienced in a very long while. I don't know.

We hardly talked except for me asking if he wanted anything from the café, and him saying a Coke, and I bought him that and a sandwich because he looked too thin. Then when he'd been seen to – only three hours, some sort of a record – I asked for his address. In the car my victim – 'Ike' he insisted, but I'm willing to bet it's 'Ian' – swore he'd learned his lesson about being rude in supermarkets, but I'm not sure he's smart enough to extend that to other shopping venues or areas of life. I've no doubt he'll be punched in the head in some pub or fast-food joint. Possibly even a Boots. Maybe church. But I told him I was glad to hear it as I drove him home, and dropped him off, and he said 'Thanks' as if I'd done him a favour, and maybe I had, and I thought that perhaps...

And I thought, after the evening's events, that *perhaps* I needed to get out of the flat because it had been too easy to do something mean just because he annoyed me. Because if I stayed there any longer on my own, it would be too easy to become a much worse person. Because if I stayed in the place where they should be but weren't and would never be again, I would just turn to stone and there was a tiny part of me that didn't want that. A tiny fluttering thing of hope locked in the Pandora's Box of me that said *Don't stay here.*

Maybe all I needed to do was get away from the Notting Hill flat with its echoes and emptiness. Maybe I wouldn't have hated it so much if I'd never had anything to compare it to. If there'd never been a before and an after. Before they left and after.

So, when I'd finishing putting everything away, I looked for the business card with its embossed gold lettering and, for better or worse, I called Albert Lowen.

~~~

Nick went shopping because I was trying to write a new novel (uncontracted).
~~~

Not even trying to finish, just trying to write, start, find a thread, a beginning, a middle, a story, whatever. And not even trying to write a line that didn't make me want to throw up when I read it over – just getting *anything* down. I was not succeeding, a thirty-five-day streak of not succeeding at the very same task, which I suppose is a sort of success. Or at least consistency.

He went to do the groceries, as simple as that, because I was trying to get some words down and it's hard to do so with a four-year-old pulling at your shirt and having a howl every five minutes about a different thing. I'd hit the point of hunching at the desk in the study nook like Gollum over his precious, trying to concentrate while a whining pierced my thin shell of calm.

'Jesus fucking Christ,' I'd muttered at last.

'If those are her next words, you're in big trouble.' Nick, from his position on the sofa in front of the TV where a football match was taking places in between a variety of faked injuries and Oscar-worthy performances, pointed a finger at me and scowled.

'How about you do something helpful? How about you go and get some food? The cupboard is bare because I'm a shit wife who forgets to shop.'

'That's true.'

'Shit wife,' echoed our child sagely.

'Maybe,' I said through gritted teeth, 'you could take our daughter with you. Have the joy of saying *no* to every lolly she reaches for, and then dealing with the fallout that will have you wishing to go back in time and have a vasectomy.'

'You'll regret those words, you know.' But he heaved himself upwards, ambled over to kiss my forehead, then gathered up the sticky-pawed fussing little girl. 'C'mon, moppet. Let's go shopping.'

'Don't forget the bags,' I said, waving vaguely towards the pantry, head back in my non-starter of a novel. Mumbling as an afterthought: 'Drive carefully.'

I didn't notice how long they were gone. Got caught up because the moment the door closed behind them, and blessed silence descended? The words arrived. Sentences and paragraphs, pages and chapters. Not beautiful, but functional – something I could polish later. As long as there was *something* there, on page, on screen, on cocktail napkin or Post-it, I could work with it. I didn't sit back and take stock until there were three messy chapters in existence, Tokyo-drifted onto the screen, and by then the sun was getting low. By then I thought they must have been elsewhere in the flat, keeping quiet so Mummy could get something done and keep her temper. Thought I'd find them in the main bedroom, on our bed, snuggled under the duvet, watching *Frozen* for the umpteenth time, and giggling together. But as I took a step to go and look, the doorbell rang, didn't it?

Two coppers, both far too young to be doing their job. They gave their names, but I cannot for the life of me recall what they were.

'Mrs Mitchell?'

'No, Dr Bainbridge. Nick Mitchell is my husband.'

They paused, obviously confused by this feminist modernity; one cleared his throat. 'Mrs – Doctor Bainbridge, there's been an accident.'

~~~

Some people might have clung to the place, closed up the doors and windows and locked themselves in with nothing but the keepsakes and recollections, watched wedding and childbirth videos ad infinitum. Buried themselves in what had once been a happy home. Practiced self-mummification. Sought a dulling of the pain with booze and pills.

Believe me, I tried.

But it was like living in an echo chamber. Every day, the vibrations of what-had-been would shudder through me, as if a train ran up and down the track of my spine sending a tremor out to each extremity. Anything I touched rang with a memory, gave me a shock like I'd grabbed a live wire. Everything hurt too much, was too intense. And we didn't have any wedding or childbirth videos anyway, and the dreams on the booze and pills were worse than anything.

By then the solicitor I didn't know Nick had, had contacted me. Details of the will. All those assets I also didn't know he had, all that money in bank accounts I never suspected. All of it mine now, or as soon as probate
~~~

was granted. None of it could replace what was gone. But I could buy a house far away from the sunny Notting Hill flat. I could buy all new furniture that had never been sat on or slept in and white goods that hadn't been leaned into to look for late-night snacks or used to wash clothes and bedding. I could sell all that or put it into storage. I could move into a hotel if it all got too much and wait it out. Could have gone shopping for new clothes. You name it, I could have bought it. Replaced it. Put all the old stuff into tidy bags and dropped it off at Oxfam, even the tiny dresses and shoes and shirts and rompers that still smelled like my little girl. The hairbrush still heavy with bright strands of strawberry red curls.

But I couldn't do that any more than I could seal up the house with myself inside it. So I was stuck in this limbo between what I was doing and what I could have done, and maybe what I should do which was probably a different thing altogether. So I stayed in the house and didn't write; deleted the file I'd been working on that day, burned the printouts of that stillborn book in the fireplace. Stayed inside and failed to see people. Left only to go shopping late at night when no one else was around and bought comfort food like a teenager with a credit card. Stayed inside and thought about how I'd not said goodbye to my daughter, not kissed her cheek one last time. Stayed in the flat and did all the stuff Albert Lowen later warned me against doing. Too little too late.

I slept downstairs in the lounge, on the sofa with a

blanket over me, a pillow that smelled like Nick under my head. I bundled up Nick's clothes and toiletries and shoes but couldn't touch Ruby's; couldn't make myself get my husband's stuff actually *out* of the house, so the bags just sat in the master bedroom, spread across the floor and the mattress. I closed the door to it and the one to Ruby's room. Closed them the day after the funeral and didn't go back in.

The only things I kept on me were the wedding and engagement bands on my finger, and a locket with a curl of Ruby's hair in it on a chain around my neck. Only those items. Keepsakes. Only those things because they were so tiny that their echoes, their pulses, their tremors were small like a low-setting flick from a tens machine trying to loosen a muscle. Manageable. Always there.

HOW I MET YOUR FATHER

In a pub, because of course it was. No dating apps for us – we'd both tried them and given up with spectacular speed. A pub meet-cute in Notting Hill, he with his friends and me with mine, too much prosecco for us, too many pints for them, and a metric shit-tonne of empty crisp packets on both tables. Tables that mysteriously and magically joined together without anyone actually seeming to move anything; a strange continental drift powered by hormones and booze.

You know, the old-fashioned way.

Five couples formed that night, remained together for varying lengths of time; there were also two one-night stands which meant at various points on the timeline we couldn't invite certain members of the friend group to certain events for fear of social discomfort and/or arguments, upset from new partners or old. Entirely too much trouble. Easier to simply do solo meet-ups or let the friendships wither. Sad but true.

It gets worse when you have children and others do not. Quite reasonably the childless don't want to discuss milestones about crawling and walking, solid food and the consistency of baby shit. And it took a while for me to notice, after the funeral, that all the friends had fallen away. Sometimes it's that you don't know what to say; you tell yourself you're respecting their privacy. Their mourning. Or maybe they thought death was something you caught; that I was a carrier.

But I digress. That night, two drunkish young people met and merged and stayed that way. He was an IT student (Masters Research) and I was working in a café to support my PhD in English Literature of the Gothic Variety habit – of the two of us, he was more likely to get a job. Me? I'd won a partial scholarship, but unless you wanted to go into academia, the snake pit of the intelligentsia, which I did not, it was a future of making coffees for me, but I was OK with that. Remaining irresponsible, I'd have all the time in the world to read books, visit galleries, libraries and museums, maybe write something. And, due to the rule of supply and demand, someone always needs someone else to make coffee.

Nick Mitchell: tall and handsome, with pale green eyes and hair black as a raven's wing, dorkily slender, but with shoulders like a coat hanger, and a ready grin that only sometimes slipped. He made me laugh and I went home with him that night, to his ground-level flat in Notting Hill, and I never really left except to get my few belongings from the house share I'd lived in for three years with a revolving door of other PhD students. If I'd given it some thought, I might have asked how an orphaned IT student could afford a flat in this district – owned it, it later transpired – but I didn't give it any thought because love hormones are also stupidity hormones; I didn't give thought to anything much but him. The sight, the feel, the smell, the sound, the everything of him. It might have simply been limerence at the start, but it turned into love and by the time the baby came along it was hard to question it, to think it might be something else. Let's face it: for the longest time life interferes with all thought.

And by the time I had started to question things, both Nick and Ruby were gone.

3

The first time I saw Albert Lowen he wore all black, was tall, thin, hollow-cheeked, red-lipped, eyes so light blue as to be almost silver, and to be honest I thought he was an undertaker drumming up business a little too late. He smelled of a pricey Tom Ford cologne and a hint of cloves. On closer inspection, the suit – handmade with stovepipe trousers (a hint of aging rock star) – was too expensive-looking, and the briefcase suggested another profession. Banker, perhaps, but he didn't quite have that avaricious air of an escaped treasury department official about him. It was worse as it turned out: solicitor. A partner at Higgins & Hyde – both of whom, he told me later, had been dead for some hundred years, but their names lived on.

'Dr Bainbridge?' he said, voice light. It was raining hard and he held an enormous umbrella, but it couldn't stop what spattered up from the flooded pavement and soaked his lower half.

I might have just stared at him. I'd buried what was left of my husband and daughter three days before and my mouth had stopped working soon after. I could hear, but every sound was noise, basically, like walking through a club when someone tries to have a conversation with you, and there's just too much static.

'Dr Everly Bainbridge?' Tone thinned to elicit a response. I think I nodded.

'I'm Albert Lowen of Higgins & Hyde, Solicitors.' He made a business card appear at the ends of his fingers as if it were a magic trick. I took it and, nerveless, dropped it into the puddle on the doorstep. He bent and picked it up, put it (oddly still dry) in my palm and closed my hand around it, like he was shutting a cage. Gave a squeeze for good measure. 'You spoke on the phone to a Mr Edwards of Addisons about your husband's estate?'

I nodded.

'I'm here to inform you that this action has been transferred to my firm. Your husband left instructions.'

I stared at him. Didn't doubt him because in the past days I'd found out my husband had lied about so many things – why wouldn't there be another surprise?

'May I come in, Dr Bainbridge?'

I found my first word in three days, spat it out: 'Why?'

'To discuss your husband's estate. Dr Bainbridge, I've sent you several emails about this.' It was like a low-level scolding from a teacher who quite liked you, was patient for the moment, but you could tell it would be a short-lived thing. 'And it's very wet out here and I would like to be less so.'

'I haven't turned the laptop on since...'

He looked me up and down with pity. 'Dr Bainbridge, is anyone here with you? Looking after you?'

I shook my head. I'd sent everyone home from the wake, remaining friends, old colleagues of Nick's. Asked to be left alone, promised I wouldn't do anything stupid, promised faithfully. And I truthfully literally hadn't done anything – neither eaten, showered nor brushed my hair or teeth, barely slept. I was still in the black dress and tights I'd worn to the funeral. No shoes, though. It was only then I became aware of how bad I smelled, old sweat and sadness.

'May I come in? Please, there are matters to be discussed.' He smiled at last, genuine, impish despite his age and the situation. 'And I'd like a cup of tea.'

To be fair, he made it himself and one for me too. He found the leftover tiny sandwiches from the wake someone (not me) had had the foresight to put in the fridge along with the other remnants. And he was wise enough to put them in the sandwich press and toast the staleness out of them so they were palatable. Then he sat and fed me bite by bite, and I didn't have the will to argue. To his credit, he didn't talk down to me, didn't suggest I take myself off and get a bit more fragrant for everyone's sake. But we stayed in the kitchen and Albert told me about my husband and exactly how much money he'd left me.

A lot more than the first solicitor had mentioned.

A metric fuck-tonne, in fact.

But it didn't matter because it simply reinforced that my husband had been a liar and kept things from me. He wasn't an orphan, but a man who'd run away from home. I should have asked more questions than I did when I met him, but there was nothing to tip me off: the flat was modest, we never lived beyond our means, the Ford was ancient, our joint bank account could have kept us out of penury for two months but no longer, we'd have been in some trouble after a bit. The advance on my first book was definitely not huge, and royalties were a tricksy and unreliable thing.

But apparently there'd been no need to have lived so small at any point in our life together. For me to have put off shopping for a week and make increasingly peculiar meals from whatever was in the cupboard and whatever hadn't turned bad in the fridge, trying to stretch the budget until this payday or that. No need to keep putting Ruby into a coat that rode up two inches from her wrists as I tried to avoid buying anything new for just a bit longer. And even later on, when we'd got a bit comfortable, the habit of frugality (worn in me like a groove in a record) meant I put off taking the Ford in for a service and new tyres for a little while...

'There are documents you need to sign, Dr Bainbridge. Are you up to it today, do you think? You should read them too.'

I stared, blinking as if it might make him go away, as if he was a smudge on the windscreen of my life and could be wiped off. Oddly, he looked younger than I'd first thought; hair not grey but an ashy blond, the face rather smooth. He cleared his throat.

‘Perhaps I’ll just leave these with you, then?’ Papers pulled from his briefcase, stacked on the table before me. ‘I’ll give you a few days, but I will be back. Is that all right?’

‘Do I have a choice?’

He shook his head, put his hands together – at first, I thought in prayer – and then cracked his knuckles. ‘No.’

I didn’t ask anything about Nick’s family, about why he’d run away, what had come between them, why he’d denied their very existence. I didn’t ask why my husband had lied to me – but then why would Albert Lowen know that? Although the solicitor certainly knew more about my husband than I did. I didn’t even see him out. Just sat there, listening to the door close, and stared at the large white envelope. ‘Higgins & Hyde’ embossed in gold in one corner, and my name in a neat script right in the centre.

When he came back at the start of the next week, I’d washed and dressed in fresh clothes, brushed my hair, eaten a few times. I don’t think I looked any better, but I didn’t look worse, and I definitely smelled better. I made him tea, me coffee, and even found some biscuits within their best-by date range in the pantry. And he told me again, who he was and who my husband was – as if I’d have forgotten in the interim – and he told me again exactly what I’d inherited. Had I made time to read the documents he’d left? Not ‘Did you manage to read?’ No. *Made time*. As if I was so very busy I had to carve out the hours.

I nodded.

Did I understand them?

I nodded.

Did I have any questions?

Shake of the head.

Would I sign everything?

I signed.

He hesitated, then asked delicately, as if walking on creaking ice: 'Would you like me to reach out to Nick's family? Arrange a meeting?'

I stared. 'Why the fuck would I want that?'

'Curiosity? But I'll take that as a no.' He slid the pages with my signature into his briefcase and rose. 'If there's anything else I can do to help, you have my number. But probate will proceed at its usual pace – are you OK, financially?'

'For the moment.'

'Higgins & Hyde will make any required funds available via bank transfer.'

'Thank you.'

This time I walked him to the door.

'Is there anything else I can do to help, Dr Bainbridge?'

'Just leave me alone.'

After he'd gone, I'd stood at the door for a while, staring at the street, at cars and houses and people and dogs walking past. Listened to the traffic and the chatter, felt the breeze on my face, and the sun. I thought about Nick and contemplated how my husband had told at least as many lies about himself as I'd told him about me.

4

To Lowen's credit, he wasn't rude or smug when I rang four months later. He wasn't annoyed that it was 2 a.m.; didn't even sound tired or as if he'd been woken. Just asked what he could do for me. Indeed, he sounded patient, as if he'd been waiting for this very call.

'Find me a new home.'

'Of course,' he replied. 'I'd suggest that you don't buy – not right now – but perhaps you'd consider a sort of a house-sit? Not that you need worry about money, but I do hate to see hasty property purchases and the market's awful at the moment. I have friends with a small place that's free, they're away for several months. That could give you some time to reflect before making any big decisions?'

'Yes,' I said, not asking where it might be because I didn't care, just reaching for whatever solution might get me out of *here*.

'Look, it's lovely and secluded. On an island off the does-what-it-says-on-the-tin town of Wells-next-the-Sea. Accessible via causeway only between mid-tide and low water. Very picturesque, I'll send you a link to the tide times.

There's the beach and the woods, so best of both worlds. Population twelve hundred, mostly clustered around the town of St Jude's to the south, but also some teeny-tiny villages and spots you'll miss if you sneeze scattered across the landscape, a few middling farms. Three point five miles long by two miles wide, four-hundred-and-fifty feet above sea level at its highest point which is a plateau at the northern tip. No castle, no cathedral due to some medieval argy-bargy, but definitely a ruined church. The house is far enough away from the main village that you won't run into anyone if you don't want to.'

His glib patter irked me. 'You sound like a travel agent – are you on commission?'

'Do you want my assistance or not?'

'Yes.' I managed to sound somewhat contrite.

'And your current flat? I can arrange for it to be leased out?'

'Just... just leave it for the moment.'

'Anything else I can help with?'

'Yes.'

~~~

A new car – had to be a new car, there was nothing left of the old Ford Mondeo – was delivered to the front door the very next morning, no questions asked, just a nice young man handing me the keys and taking away the rental. Several hours later – because leaving was harder than I thought – I set off in a north-eastish direction
~~~

(third star to the left and all that shit) in a shiny blue Mercedes-AMG SL63, to a house with no echoes. Or not my echoes, at least.

The trip takes more of the day than I'd prefer but I also know the next low tide will be at 11.15 tonight so I make a lot of stops, stare at landmarks and ruins and things with plaques on them. I avoid services and find cafés instead. It's summer and the sun's long-lasting, so even though I'm in the car for what feels like forever there's still some fleeting light when I arrive at Wells-next-the-Sea, which is pretty, its beach home to colourful bathing huts; no one's about. Across the bay is St Jude's Isle. It doesn't take me long to find the causeway.

It's almost a ten-minute drive, and the village of St Jude's looks as picturesque as Albert Lowen said. Or as much of it as I can see this late. Neat and tidy; a Midsomer-somewhere-to-get-murdered type of tidy. No litter on the streets, hedges uniformly straight, manicured lawns and pretty stone houses painted white or pink or yellow or blue, windows sparkling clean, thatch all refreshed, storefronts bright, no potholes in the roads, garden gates perfectly in alignment, roses growing up and over trellises for best display. All ducks in a row. Or so it seems in the flicker of my headlights, the random streetlights. Everything is a flashing blur, so who am I kidding?

I don't stop. I make note of the cafés (three) and the pubs (two), the corner store-cum-post office (one) for future reference, because when Lowen texted me the location he said that the pantry would be full. I drive past a compact council chambers and a library, a school building, a clothing store and what looks like a hippy shop advertising tarot readings. The GPS on my phone keeps me going for another fifteen minutes until I come to a high stone wall that runs along Martham Road for a while. At last, there's a black iron barrier (considerably newer than the wall), a keypad and intercom on a wooden post to the right and a brass plate that says 'Morningthorpe', all lit by a strip of solar lights. I punch in the code Albert sent, wait as the gates open silently and then wonder, as I take in the gatehouse to my left and the very long driveway ahead of me, what the hell I've got myself into.

At the end of said driveway, which weaves through thick woods, I slow considerably because everything the high beams hit seems to strobe in front of me, that sensation increases one hundred-fold.

It's not a 'house-sit', it's a fucking 'mansion-sit'.

A sandstone rectangle, fifteen sash windows across, huge front door, steps leading up to it from a formal garden. Two storeys, an attic with dormers, a half-basement the windows of which just peek above the manicured lawn. And floodlights springing to life to illuminate the façade as I park out front.

'No one will bother you there,' Albert had said. 'Perfect quiet. You might be able to get some perspective on things. Remember, I'm just a phone call away, don't hesitate to ring, day or night.'

Which is what I do – the ringing, not the hesitating.

'What,' I ask as soon as he picks up, 'the fuck is this?'

'You've arrived, I take it.'

'Albert, this isn't a house. This isn't a flat. This is definitely not a loaner. This is the sort of place that gets rented out on Airbnb for four days for roughly the GNP of a small African nation powered by conflict diamonds.' I stare through the windscreen as if the looming structure outside, the stone statues and wooden benches, raised garden beds and blooming curtains of jasmine around the fountain might disappear if I wish hard enough.

'Are you worried about money? Because–'

'I'm not worried about money, Albert, although I'm sure the cost would be obscene. This is a... palace.' I hiss the last word.

'Well, technically no. It's a country house, the sort rich people generally own in concert with a townhouse and possibly a pied-à-terre in Paris.'

'I hate you so much.'

'There you go! There's some passion in you yet, that rage. Hang on to that, it's always very useful for climbing out of pits, emotional, physical, spiritual, mental.'

'Albert—'

'Look, it's a bolthole, OK? A really big one, I concede that, but it's a place to stay away from everyone and everything. You're not surrounded by all the old sad things. It's a new location and you're the only old sad thing there. Just give it a few days.' He clears his throat. 'I know it's hard, Everly, grief is hard. It clings – as it should, I suppose, that's how you know you're not a sociopath – it takes time to either get through or become accustomed to. You know how Emily Dickinson said hope is the thing with feathers? Well, grief is the thing with claws. It takes a while, and some people don't survive it. But you, Everly Bainbridge, I think you're special. You're a survivor. So, settle in, pick the prettiest bedroom, sleep, have a walk in the morning, go to one of the cafés and have scones. The coffee is awful in all three of them, by the way – this is England – but the scones are *lovely*. Read a book. Cry. Wait. Life will happen whatever you do. Key's under the mat. Off you go now.'

And the bastard hangs up on me.

I get out of the car, and grab my suitcase, handbag and laptop satchel. I leave the Mercedes slewed on the gravel driveway – the gates slid closed behind me when I drove through, and we're on an island, who's going to steal it? And, for fuck's sake, when I check the mat at the front door, the house key is indeed there – big and iron and roughly made, nothing like the high-tech gates. I slide it into the lock; before I turn it, though, I take one final look back at the car.

There it is, all alone. Then from the corner of my eye, however, I spy something drifting along that uncertain boundary where the formal gardens and pristine avenues shift between the glare of the floodlights and the shadowy woods. Or I think there is. A giggle reaches me, or I think it does: the glee of a child who's playing hide-and-seek. My hand goes to the locket at my throat, feels the pulse inside. I blink.

It – whatever it was or is, or whatever I imagined – is gone. A fat squirrel appears in its place. Shaking my head, I swallow to try and clear the lump in my throat. Terrific. Hallucinations. Just what I need to fill the hole in my heart. I'm not, I'm surprised to find, afraid; just so terribly sad.

'You weren't ever *here*,' I whisper to the garden, the squirrel, the misty shifty thing. 'You never came to this place. You aren't here now. Mummy's just going nuts.'

And I face the door once again, turn the key, hear the thud and snap of the latch. The lion-headed doorknob twists of its own accord and judders backwards even though I don't push it.

Air, icy and damp and with a hint of mildew rushes out.

Old houses often have bad breath.

I step over the threshold into a marble hall, and as soon as my foot hits the tiles, low warm light spills from the lamps around the room. Handy. But it can't dispel the chill. Black and white chequered tiles, wood panelling, family portraits from different eras, their subjects with chins in various stages of receding, marble plinths topped with bronze busts, a hall table in even more marble with gilt legs and embellishments.

I push the door closed behind me, then wait, listening, leaning against the sturdy wood.

Nothing.

There's no one else here, the entire gigantic building is empty, just as Albert Lowen said.

I leave my suitcase at the base of the stairs, then set off along the corridor to the left, down a short set of steps and into the kitchen, which is enormous, as if meant to feed huge families and feudal followers and retinues; I calculate it's actually a half-basement. Not new but renovated maybe in the last ten years. More black and white tiles, snowy cupboards, butcher's block countertops and an island with five long-legged stools. A locked door in the far wall that I can only assume leads to the sub-cellar. Maybe they lock up the wine or the Amontillado. Industrial lighting that looks odd. There's a huge Aga in a recessed nook that was probably once the main fireplace, crockery cupboards, pots and pans hanging from a wooden framework above the island. In the pantry – there are two, in fact – and fridge is enough food to feed an army. A bowl beside the farmhouse sink is piled high with fresh fruit. I take an apple, find a packet of chocolate digestives in the cupboard, a small wheel of Roquefort cheese, make a cup of hot chocolate and sit on one of those tall stools.

I finish the biscuits and half the cheese. When I try to log on to the laptop, I realise Albert never gave me the Wi-Fi details. There's a network there, I can see it. I think about hot-spotting to my phone, then realise I don't care enough to do it. There's nothing I want to check, no emails I want to answer, no social media I want to engage with; that this is all pure habit. That being away from home has kicked in some of my forgotten behaviours because they're things that feel like a routine I once had, and in an unfamiliar place I reach for that routine for comfort. I turn the laptop off.

Filled with cheese and regret, I head back upstairs to find the prettiest bedroom as instructed.

5

The first room – the master suite – had its cupboards half-filled with clothes, and I didn't think the owners would appreciate me snuggling up in their bed. The second one I tried had the décor for a teenage boy, so no thank you. The third was juuuuust right – if you like a lot of florals and pink wallpaper, which I don't, but beggars can't be choosers and I was too exhausted to continue the search. Anyway, the queen-size bed was comfortable, there was a clawfoot bath in the adjoining en suite, and the cupboards were bare.

I wish I could say I slept well. I slept dead but didn't wake at all refreshed. Can't remember my dreams either, which is unusual for me; I generally rise with the embers of them burning in me or their wisps drifting across my eyes like silken cobwebs. Nothing, either good or bad. Given the amount of cheese I had before bed, it's a miracle.

Awake, if not alert, I have a shower and put on clothes that hopefully don't make me look entirely homeless. Grab my handbag. When I step outside, I find three very late season bluebells on the mat. They must have blown in from somewhere in the woods. I set them to the side so I don't step on them when I return later.

~~~

Before I can locate one of the cafés, I spot the church's spire. It's not far from the village and I don't know how I missed it last night; it was late, I suppose, and you forget how bloody dark anything that's not the city is. Parking, I drift towards it. Hard to resist architecture no matter how bad you're feeling, and I'm not starving, still a bit cheese-queasy if I'm honest. The churchyard is immaculately tended, the grass over the weathered graves manicured even though the headstones tilt to the side or backwards or forwards, like drunks trying to remain upright in order to pass a sobriety test. A large yew tree grows right beside the church's north wall, its branches reaching across the roof.

The building is small, ancient, its stained-glass windows a bit dull but I guess they're leery of cleaning them lest they break. I step onto the little portico to examine the door, which isn't exactly typical: it's not banded with iron like most of its age and type but looks no less venerable. It's a single piece of wood, no sign of joins, and the carving is what grabs my interest: a tree with a rope hanging from a branch and a man suspended from the noose.

I reach out, barely touch the contours before the thing creaks back as if shimmying away, and a puff of air escapes; similar to that at the house, but older, even
~~~

more stale, like... grave dirt. Which should be a warning, let's face it, but there's an opening and here's me with an unhealthy dose of curiosity paired with a dreadful numbness in my soul. I push my way in, the fingers of one hand on my locket, the others on the wood which feels terribly cold.

It's very dim, even the light through the stained-glass windows seems dialled down. I close my eyes, trying to become accustomed to the shadows; it helps a little but not enough. The torch on my phone cuts a swathe through the darkness. Rows of dusty pews, a central aisle of cracked flagstones, fractures going though engraved names and dates to make a puzzle of the dead and buried. Niches cut into the walls with burned-down candles leaning tipsily in them; bits of furniture pushed against said walls, partially covered in old floral sheets. Pillars holding up the vaulted ceiling, stone-carved roses looking down, traces of old gilt and faded colours from the place's heyday. A small pulpit to one side, its elaborate canopy says that once this church was very well patronised by whatever rich family or families held sway over St Jude's Isle. In the distance, a tumble of books – hymnals – and what appear to be second-hand pulp novels – has cascaded off a low chest of drawers backed against the rood screen that protects (very inefficiently) the chancel from prying eyes; tomes litter the floor like stepping stones.

The smell of grave dirt grows stronger the further I

move in, which would be because of the great hole in the crossing; it eats the light from my torch and I'm not sure what's down there. I stop where the thick, dusty splintered boards criss-cross the abyss (I'm not stupid enough to test them) and stare across at the altar. A once-white cloth greyed with dust, edges embroidered with what looks like holly and crucifixes and silver dots, is hung rather short so it doesn't obscure the bas-relief front of the stone altar. It's identical to the door: tree, rope, branch, man.

The boards creak even though there's no weight on them. I think I've seen enough. It's deathly quiet, so when there's a voice behind me, even though it's only saying *Hello*, I jump and swear.

'Jesus fucking Christ!'

'Judas Iscariot, actually.' The woman's in jeans, a black shirt with a dog collar, and a bright pink cardigan, hands in pockets. Black hair, short with streaks of grey, great skin and eyes that might be green, but who can tell in this light? Tall and loose-limbed. 'Sorry, vicar humour.'

'Never mind the dog collar, you need a bell, warn people you're coming. Don't go sneaking around the countryside, scaring folk.'

She lifts a foot, shows off her shoes. 'Sneakers, for the sneaking.'

'Right.' I gesture around us. 'Yours?'

'Yes. Or in as much as one owns such a place.' She smiles. 'We don't use it. Too expensive to fix what ails it.

Kept as a curiosity, but no one's supposed to be in here because, well, danger.'

'It was unlocked,' I say, trying not to sound defensive. Trying not to say *It invited me in* because that honestly sounds a bit like *It was asking for it*.

'I believe you. The lock's dodgy. But again, no money to fix anything.' She holds out a hand. 'I'm Amelia Willoughby.'

'Vicar Amelia. I'm Everly.'

'I'd offer you a tour but I think you've already had one. Unless you're committed to looking at the crypt?'

'Absolutely fucking not. I mean, no thank you. As I said, it was unlocked and I was curious, but big dark holes in the ground are not of interest. Thank you.'

'Not a tourist, then?'

'Not willingly. I'm... staying nearby for a bit. I was in search of scones,' I say lamely, not wanting to explain everything. I point at the altar carving. 'Judas Iscariot, you say? Interesting choice.'

She nods. 'It's a very old church – I know there are a lot of medieval signifiers, but there's evidence it was here well before that period, maybe that it was something else entirely – and people have their own interpretations of the Bible. Some thought that he did what was needed – without him, nothing else happens, the church doesn't get its greatest martyr – that's Jesus by the way – or its grand revolution to the idea of a merciful God. Judas took one for the team, so to speak, and is therefore rather necessary and deserving of worship.'

'One way of looking at it,' I say, but bite down on the words *If you believe in that sort of thing*. 'You also seem a bit undersubscribed to traditional theology for a vicar. I mean, you don't sound outraged?'

She shrugs. 'Outrage is exhausting, don't you find? I think religion should be about looking after people, when they're living. The spiritual stuff, if we're right, will take care of itself later – but if you don't feed and clothe and house people? Give comfort when they're grieving? It's really hard to expect them to have faith in a better world when they're hungry and homeless and naked and heartsick. Why should they subscribe to the idea that they're born to suffer?'

'Rebel. Bet you start fist fights at synods.'

She snorts. 'Sorry, high horse. I believe you mentioned something about scones?' I nod. 'Come on, then, I'll show you to the best café – the coffee is universally terrible. And remember that everyone has strong feelings about whether the cream or jam goes first depending on which county you're in – stronger than their religious convictions in many cases – and you'd best do it right or they'll talk about you. For the record, jam first around here.'

'My sense is that people talk about you no matter what you do, scone-related or otherwise, no matter where you are.'

'True.' She moves aside and sweeps her hand towards the open door and the path of sunlight that awaits just outside. I take a step, hear the click of my heel on the floor and feel disoriented – had my footsteps sounded before, when I entered? When I walked along the aisle? I genuinely can't remember; all I recall is the treacle-heavy silence, the lack of noise from outside. Not even birdsong, nor traffic. But as I get close to the exit, those two sounds swell, and my footfall is loud. As if the church, left to its own devices, ate the noise.

To distract myself, I ask: 'So if the church isn't in use where do you do your vicar-ing?'

'I cover four small parishes, alternating Sunday sermons. We live here – I was born here.' She points vaguely in the direction of a very tall hedge, behind which I assume is a parsonage. 'There's a small church near the northern tip, and then three others on the mainland that are mine. Most folk on St Jude's don't bother, but the low-key do once a month, and the truly committed do the circuit.'

I laugh.

'Here, I'm just a sort of caretaker, stopping wandering women from falling into crypts.' She pulls the door shut behind us, and the lock *thunks* into place. Amelia shakes the handle; it doesn't shift and she gives a satisfied nod.

Outside, the day's become very warm, very bright; it's an out-of-the-tomb experience. I pause for a moment, raise my face to the sun and bask, eyes closed, until the vicar's gentle touch is on my elbow, only for a second, but it's enough to get me moving, doing my best to forget the church is behind me, it also with a great hole in its heart.

Few remember that an apocalypse is more than mere destruction. Its original meaning is to reveal, uncover, or disclose. Laying bare hard and painful truths is therefore a matter of light and its application.

ANEURIN BEDDOE, Doctor Theologiae,
Aspects of Etymological Excavation, 1932 A.D.

6

Mabel's looks out over the bay, and is filled with rickety-looking chairs, and tables covered by hand-embroidered cloths with glass vases in the centre, each holding a different variety of pink flower. There are three customers already, women in their fifties or thereabouts: one in a yellow twin set and tweed skirt is reading a paper; another in jodhpurs, riding boots and a washed-thin sweater stares out the window; and the third in dark jeans, fancy-looking wellies and a blue linen shirt who's reading a novel with a lurid cover (not mine). The counter and fridge cabinet are packed with an assortment of cakes and sweets and scones – more than the current café population could get through, which suggests they get a good deal more tourist traffic than it would appear.

Amelia calls 'Hello, Mabel' to the woman at the coffee machine; pale lilac apron over a floral frock, half-moon glasses, soft brown hair tied in a bun at the base of her neck and a little off to the side like a 1930s 'do. No make-up, late forties. She smiles. No one else looks up.

'Hello, Amelia, who's your friend?' The proprietor's

got a melodious voice, almost sounds like she's singing as she gives the vicar a cursory glance and me a once-over. 'What'll it be this morning?

'This is Everly. Scones, please, Mabel, and tea for two. We'll be outside.'

The vicar leads me into a paved courtyard, its roof made up of climbing vines and a framework. I can smell the sea although I can't see it from here. An almost-perfect summer retreat. Amelia chooses the table furthest from the door and makes small talk until Mabel brings out the best scones and jam I've ever had, and a pot of tea.

'And in case I wasn't clear, don't order the coffee. Ever,' warns Amelia as she pours. 'I mean, it's meant to be bitter, but there are limits.'

'Not to be rude, but shouldn't you,' I ask, 'be vicar-ing?'

'I am.' She gestures at me. 'You look terrible. Ministering to a flock doesn't just mean the ones you know. It means randoms you find on the church steps as well, or wandering inside. Again, you look terrible, soul-sick.' She shrugs. 'I could be wrong, this could just be a dreadful hangover – but you look hollow and lost and generally awful.'

'Work a lot with depressed people, do you?'

'Well, I start but then they run away...'

I find myself laughing. Not just the sort of snort I've developed the past months, but an actual belly laugh. And then I feel guilty because my husband and child are gone and I'm here and I'm eating scones and laughing in the sun. And that's when I start to cry. Snot, hiccups and all. The vicar hands over a large clean men's hanky. I tell her, in between tears and a bit of dribble, everything that happened – to Nick and Ruby, to me, even about Ike and the shopping trolley and what a shit person I've become (or always was but managed to cover up until recently).

When I'm done, Vicar Amelia says, 'I can't tell you when or if you'll ever feel better. And there's no timeline – you're not underachieving in the grief Olympics. There're no developmental milestones you need to hit. Just be kind to yourself. Rest. Read. Stare into space. Take walks, eat scones. If the urge strikes, start writing again. Doesn't have to be the next book, could just be letters. Ones you don't send. Might just be to yourself, because everything that's inside you? It'll go sour if you don't let it out.'

'Lumpy milk of human kindness.'

'Precisely. Even if you're just speaking those things aloud, it's a release. And they do need to get out, trust me. Got a mobile?' We swap numbers. 'Ring or text whenever you need to. And you should come to dinner. My wife will be delighted to cook for someone who's not bored with her usual repertoire.'

'Thank you,' I say. 'I won't return your hanky.'

'I appreciate that.' She grins.

I stretch in my chair and take a deep breath, look around. In the doorway, the woman in the blue linen shirt is watching us. A soon as I catch her eye, and offer a smile, she ducks back inside. Ah, isolated location suspicion. *A local shop for local people* rings in my head. Amelia and I talk for another hour or so, then she has to head off for an appointment. After she leaves, I scour the last of the scone crumbs from my plate before settling the bill (the original customers have gone, five new ones including three men have taken their place) and having a leisurely walk to where I parked the car by the church, which I have no urge to revisit.

Starting the ignition, I feel better, somehow; not good, but lighter. The guilty part of me says it's too soon. Too soon to feel not so shit. The other part, the bit that Amelia spoke to, that listened to her, says it's OK. I say it out loud 'It's OK not to feel so shit,' and my voice in the confined space sounds louder than it should, has more conviction, and I don't entirely misbelieve it.

~~~

Back in the mansion, in the kitchen, I set myself up with the laptop, wrap a thick cardigan around me for warmth. Something about my conversation with the vicar has inspired me to write, and if I learned anything with the first book it was to go with that feeling. It won't always be there and you'll have to write anyway – but when it's there the ride is smoother.

I don't try to rewrite the book that died when my family did. Instead I reach back to the first novel, to the memory of its creation – picking the flesh from the bones
~~~

of its truth, remaking that flesh into something else – and think of how that pulled me from the edge. How it helped to make living and breathing and pretending to be normal just a bit easier. When the nightmares of my first life had resurfaced I was pregnant with Ruby, and I didn't want her to be infected by them, so I put them onto the page. Not the whole story, not the entire truth, but a reshaping of it.

So now, I take the second story of my life – the second terrible story – and begin to craft it into something with its feet in truth but growing it into a new and dreadful shape, putting my suffering *away* from me. That's what writing is: turning what happened into a lie so no one but you recognises it. Same as I did with the first terrible life. I write in a fever as if the faster I write, the further I'll be from that moment, from that awful day. I write until I fall asleep – I don't remember it, but I must have, right? – fall asleep at the kitchen island, head pillowed on my outstretched arm beside the laptop, the low whir a lullaby.

I wake with no memory of anything – for a moment I'm utterly blank. Neither name nor recollections to weigh me down and I feel so light that I almost take a step forwards, convinced I can fly. Then an echo comes, a small voice behind me, calling 'Mummy'. A small voice that no longer exists, yet nearly drops me in my tracks.

The smell of dirt and damp and old things. Maybe a hint of meat, but it's gone quickly, so quickly I'm not sure it was ever there.

I've got one foot lifted off the ground, the other... the grip of my sneaker is precarious, near the edge of... something. Bricks, curved and cold. All my awareness abruptly returns and I pat my cardigan pockets (Balance! Balance! Balance!), looking for that smooth rectangle of comfort; find my mobile in the right one. Light pours out, the torch app saving me from myself.

There's a hole in front of me: a well, an oubliette, a circle of impenetrable blackness, straight down. A dark echo of the church today. I stumble back, fall away from the gaping maw, hit the floor, jarring my tailbone. The hurt wakes me properly, centres me and pulls me back from the panic. Straightening, I train the beam around me. A room stacked with wine racks and shelves, dusty barrels and crates. And there's a light source, I now realise, not just my phone. Behind me: a door maybe ten metres away at the top of a flight of stairs, and naked bulbs leading the way up. The brilliant glare of the kitchen beyond.

That's when the fear grips me and I scramble upright, half-run, half-walk away from the hole in the floor, up the stairs and fall into the kitchen. I kick the door shut.

The locked door I'd noticed the night I arrived. *Locked.*

There's a key sticking in the lock – which I must have

put there in the first place? But where did I find it? I turn it, hear the mechanism engage, remove that key and fold it into my palm, then flee up to my room, slam that door, lock it, sit on the bed, breathing hard.

I'll deal with it all in the morning.

I could leave.

I should leave.

Pack up and find a hotel, a B&B; sit in a brightly lit services by the side of a motorway and watch traffic go by. Phone Albert Lowen at 2 fucking a.m. again and yell at him.

But I can't. I can't because of one tiny thing.

That small voice that shouldn't exist.

Mummy.

But I take the key over to the window and throw the thing out with all my might.

7

My mobile buzzes while I'm having coffee the next morning, sitting at a green metal table and chair in the small walled garden outside the kitchen; not *in* the kitchen because I'm still spooked about it. About its proximity to that cellar, even though I locked the door and threw away the key. Even though when I checked it this morning it was still thoroughly, emphatically locked. Haven't even had food yet, not even fruit, because I keep revisiting last night's adventure and it makes me sick to my stomach. What do they say? *It's not the fall that kills you...*

What if I'd not woken in time?

What if I'd taken that final step?

How far down?

What would have happened if I'd fallen?

What would have happened when I hit?

How long would it have been?

What if I'd died on impact?

What if I didn't?

The same sort of thoughts as those that have plagued me on and off since childhood. What if *he* hadn't? And what if *I* didn't? I shake my head, circle back to *now*.

What about that voice?

Who'd have found me?

Anyone?

Why would there be a big fucking black hole in the family wine cellar?

Maybe, I say reasonably, no one was expected to be here; maybe the family know best how to walk around it, like a creaking step on a staircase in a house you've inhabited for thirty years. Maybe Albert didn't know about the big fucking black hole?

Would Albert Lowen have come looking?

Part of me wants to call him, tell him what happened, but the other part doesn't want anyone to know. I've not sleepwalked in years, not since I was pregnant. There were reasons for that then, but...

Well, maybe there *is* a perfectly good reason to start sleepwalking. And hearing voices. But maybe I don't need or want anyone to know that what happened most recently is having an effect on me. This *particular* effect.

The mobile buzzes again and again, like a series of random thoughts being blurted out. The name AMELIA flashes, then four messages, all caps:

HELLO!

DINNER TONIGHT?

CARRIE KEEN TO MEET U.

BIT OF A DO ON THE COMMON AFTER. LOCAL COLOUR.

Then: Sorry, caps lock attack.
I reply: Maypoles or Morris dancers?

SURPRISE. Poss some dncg, but no maypoles and defs no Morris. Promise.

She gives an address and time as if my agreement is a foregone conclusion. Maybe it is.

The exchange has the advantage of breaking my spiral. I shower, dress and begin working well before lunchtime (although not in the kitchen). I set myself up in the library, pulling back the thick blue chintz curtains on every window to let the light in, the risk of fading sunshine be damned. Sitting at the large mahogany desk with its banker's lamp and blotter, the comfort of all those bookshelves at my back like soldiers at attention, the scents of paper and leather and the lemongrass tea I made wafting around. Tearing through more chapters, I use last night's true nightmare as a plot point, pouring my terror onto the page until it doesn't make me quite so sick to think of the possibilities. I write through lunch and keep going, once again feverish, for most of the day until the alarm on my phone sounds and it's time to make myself presentable.

I drive into the village, the GPS leading directly to a

neat red-brick vicarage, considerably more modern than I expected, behind which I can see the hedge and the tip of the church's tower. Standing in the driveway, still staring, I don't hear the front door open.

'Hello!' Not Amelia. The woman's shorter, dark olive skin, greying hair reaching to her shoulders. A pair of beige wide-legged trousers so elegantly cut that they can't have come off-the-rack, and a sage-coloured shirt with no hint of a wrinkle. Not my picture of a vicar's wife, but then I'm not sure I'd ever bothered to picture a vicar's wife before. She calls, 'I'm Carrie. Carrie Hainford. Dr. So lovely to meet you.'

'Bainbridge. Everly. Dr. Hello.' I hold up the bottles I pilfered from the wine rack: a Santa Duc Châteauneuf-du-Pape 'Habemus Papam' 2019 and a Domaine Jean Noël Gagnard Clos de la Maltroye Premier Cru, Chassagne-Montrachet 2020. Both of which cost more than I've ever spent on booze in my entire life (I googled), but Albert Lowen did tell me to make myself at home. 'I wasn't sure if you were a red or white household?'

Carrie whistles. 'We're non-denominational in this respect. You can come again.'

'It's stolen,' I confess.

'Oh well, say three something-somethings, hand over the booze and all your sins shall be forgiven.' She takes the red and waves me into the house.

The conversation flows freely, the food is good and simple: roast chicken and vegetables, apple pie and ice cream for pudding. I give Ike a brief thought, hope he's still intact and hasn't started a fight with some psycho in the fruit and veg section because the chances of him being beaten to death with an aubergine were not zero.

We talk about things that don't involve dead children and lying husbands, and that's a relief. About how they met, how Amelia used to be a university lecturer before she found vicar-hood; how Carrie still lectures on comparative religions, staying three days a week in Cambridge, coming home to St Jude's for four. I do my best to ask most of the questions so that the attention stays firmly on them; although Amelia had obviously told Carrie everything she'd learned so no one digs into my past, which is a relief.

'Everly,' says Carrie with a little hiccup. 'What a beautiful name.'

'Don't get too carried away,' I say. 'It means "boar in a meadow".'

We fall about laughing. Once recovered, I offer to do the dishes.

'No, no,' says Amelia. 'That can wait. Besides Carrie is the dishwasher stacker, no one else can do it properly.'

'Don't hate me for my gift,' says Carrie, rising. 'My wife's right, though bitter. Plus, we need to get along to the surprise.'

I groan. 'It's a Morris dancing flash mob, isn't it.'

'You shouldn't be so rude about them.' Amelia waves a finger. 'The god of Morris dancers will smite thee...'

'Oh, don't get her started. C'mon. I'll tell a story on the way.'

Outside, the air is cool and sobering. Amelia directs us towards a gentle incline and soon we're climbing a small hill. Carrie begins: 'Don't know if Amy told you, but I'm a glutton for folklore. There's the tale of the Straw Witch of St Jude's. Do you know it?'

'Safe to say I do not.'

'The straw witch was a poor woman, homeless, who scraped a living by selling charms and begging what food she could – and if folk were in a good mood, they were sometimes kind. She would sleep in haylofts and barns whenever she could, to simply keep out of the elements. Some farmers didn't mind, some did, so she had to be careful where she lay, and whether she was seen. Such sleeping arrangements meant she always had straw on her person whether she liked it or not, and she found a use for it, twisting stray pieces into talismans and corn dollies. Little things she could sell. At first, she was called the straw dam, harmless enough, until one of the women who'd bought a charm miscarried. Terribly sad, but people are always looking for someone to blame – no one can bear the idea that shit sometimes just happens—'

'Inspiring words from a vicar's wife.'

'You get used to it,' says Amelia, and sighs.

Carrie continues '—shit sometimes just happens. This woman claimed it was the straw *witch* who'd done it. That the woman had been sold a cursed thing to do her harm. Well, you know how hysteria moves, and soon there was a wave of complaints to the local constable, priest and lord – she'd hexed this thing and that; someone's sheep died after she passed the fold; a field grew barren when she set foot on in; someone's cows stopped giving milk; butter had magically disappeared from the churn while she stood outside the farmhouse; someone else felt pain in their toe when the straw witch stubbed *hers* so clearly she was "throwing" hurt. They put her on trial, and she was found innocent by the magistrate on the mainland – there's something new and rare, right? But when freed she came back here, it was her home she thought, and that night, when she found a barn to sleep in, someone they say set it on fire.'

'Jesus.'

'Lord's name in vain,' Amelia says mildly, puffing a little as we hit the halfway mark, and the incline gets a little steeper.

'*Anyway*, she dies. Dies horribly, this poor woman who's done no harm to anyone – and whose name is lost because no one cared enough to write down anything but "the straw witch". The village goes back to normal, everyone thinks they're safe and sound now this dangerous homeless woman is gone.'

'Except...'

'Except, people start burning in their beds. The houses are fine, their mattresses a little smouldery but intact, but inhabitants are found the next day as roasts. And what do folk start saying is wandering the night, all along the cobbled streets?'

'A straw witch?'

'Precisely. A woman made out of straw, no face to be seen, just a black absence in the head of what looks like a giant corn dolly. And they say *she* burns without being consumed.'

'Fascinating,' I say, 'but what's this got to do with— Oh, shit, you're not going to Wicker Man me, are you?'

'How rude,' grumbles Amelia.

'Very rude indeed,' agrees her wife with a sniff. 'No, but tonight is the night when the locals burn an effigy and ask her to leave the village alone.'

'And you're OK with this?' I look at Amelia.

She shrugs. 'Everly, down that hill is a church dedicated to Judas Iscariot. This little vestige of the past? It's sort of a reminder not to be mean, isn't it? I've never thought it's a good idea to other those who believe differently – what's the point? That's not religion, that's a power play. Inclusivity, m'dear, is the watchword.'

Carrie rushes ahead. 'Hurry up, you two, we'll miss the start!'

8

At the top of the hill – it can hardly be called a hill, more a bump in the landscape – there's a flat, neatly mowed meadow, thick trees surrounding three sides. A decent-sized crowd has gathered, adults and children, chatting and laughing, relaxed. Some have camping chairs, others lounge on picnic blankets. A couple of trestle tables hold cakes and plastic cups, a couple of punchbowls and three of those thermal urns. In the centre of it all, an effigy.

A corn dolly.

Almost twice my height, an intricate weaving of straw with wildflowers threaded through for a riot of colour spiralling around and down the body, a line of purple-blue is particularly vibrant.

'What do you think?' asks Carrie.

'That bluebells are out of season?'

'There's always some to be found for this.' Carrie grins.

'So, what's this for? Is the day relevant? The day the straw witch was burned?'

'On or around – it's not recorded, a general time of "the first week in June". This is just a little thing, a St Jude's Isle celebration to pay our respects and ask her to forgive what our ancestors did.'

'By burning her again?' I ask tentatively.

Carrie fixes me with a frank gaze. 'Look, if you're going to apply cold logic to our ancient traditions, you're not going to enjoy this very much. Nor am I for that matter.'

I raise my hands in surrender.

'Help me with these, you pair. Hot hot hot.' Amelia, who'd made a beeline for the beverage tables, is holding three cups with teabag tails hanging from them. 'Biscuits in my left pocket, darling.'

Armed with cups of scalding tea and slightly crushed jammy dodgers, we drift closer to the corn dolly. Soon enough a short, red-haired woman in a flowing purple cheesecloth dress ('Owns the local spooky store,' Amelia whispers, 'Amphillis "Hates being called Phillis" Caston.') makes her way to the centre of the meadow carrying a torch – the old-fashioned sort, one end wrapped in charcloth. I get a whiff of kerosene on the evening breeze. There's a succinct speech about the straw witch, a tiny potted history version of what Carrie told me and which surely everyone else already knows, then Amphillis digs out a gold cigarette lighter from somewhere in her bra and lights the torch, which flares to life with an audible *whumph*.

She touches the burning brand to the tinder at the foot of the corn dolly and soon there's a loud crackling sound as the flames devour the effigy. The bluebells and other flowers wilt quickly but take longer to burn, still green as they are. The whole conflagration doesn't take long, relatively speaking, and when it's done everyone drifts away. No need to worry. Nothing like a cult. Nothing like the one I'd known.

We return to the vicarage, and Amelia says, 'If you don't feel up to driving – we did drink a lot – you're welcome to the couch. The spare room's still full of boxes from our move seven years ago. My not-so-secret shame.'

I'm about to refuse politely, then I think about the big empty house, about the cellar and the pit. About the little voice that shouldn't be there. I say, 'Thank you. The couch would be great.'

It's only after the lights are turned out and the couple make their way upstairs and I'm stretched on the comfortable-all-things-considered couch beneath an alpaca wool blanket that a thought hits and knocks the breath from me.

For a few hours I forgot about everything. I forgot about my child and my husband and the trainwreck of my life. For a few hours, I enjoyed the company of others, thought about things other than death. For a few hours I laughed carelessly.

And I'm overwhelmed with guilt and sorrow and cry myself to sleep.

〰〰〰

RING, RING

Kensington and Chelsea Register Office, Chelsea Old Town Hall, afternoon, 1 May, 20–

I'm wearing a short guipure lace vintage dress, off-white or maybe intentionally cream – hard to tell with a sixties piece – from Camden Market, new high red boots, a bouquet of lilac roses, a veil borrowed from a friend and underneath it all a pair of blue knickers. Nick's in a second- or third-hand suit, Savile Row, but definitely with some miles on it. We've been together for three years now, he's graduated and working for an IT company, writing software. It's a regular wage, he seems to like it or at least doesn't complain about going every day.

My PhD is sliding glacially towards a conclusion – every time I read something new and the glacier grinds to a halt, for just a while until I sort out my thoughts on 'a fresh angle' on gothic girls and the crushing weight of the patriarchy, about going kicking and screaming to some place you didn't want to and then, rebelling instead of quietly becoming a wife, mother, a sacrifice, and pretending to be contented when you were really starting to understand the mad woman in the attic wasn't actually mad at all. It's fine. I'm still making coffee – I like making coffee – but in a different café now. Dealing with people is always a challenge; there are regulars and I like them and mostly I manage to not tell a dickhead to fuck right off.

It's fine. It's normal and ordinary, and I'd had more than enough of not-normal and not-ordinary for the first thirteen years of my life.

Anyway, there we were in the registry office, two old friends as witnesses, no family because orphans. A few weeks before, he'd handed me a very large ring which he said had been his grandmother's, a gigantic diamond that might have bought us an actual London house or an entire small village somewhere else. He'd said there'd been money in the family once, and now all that boiled down to was this particular diamond and its peculiar frigidity. And it was so huge, I didn't really like it on my skinny finger. And it was so cold, that it gave me chills, never taking on the warmth of my flesh. And it was so heavy, I felt I was dragging around the weight of a dead grandmother and someone else's extinct family. But it was also so fucking expensive and rare that I couldn't take it off for fear I'd lose it, leave it somewhere, that we'd get robbed and some spotty teen burglar would nick it and pawn it for fifty quid.

So, I wore the damned thing like an obligation because I did want to marry Nick and I didn't want to hurt him, and eventually the weight felt normal and it only bothered me sometimes. I guess that's how cognitive dissonance works.

I wake before dawn, feeling thick-headed and generally *meh*, but it doesn't stop me from quietly letting myself out of the vicarage. I hope Amelia and Carrie didn't hear me weeping last night – don't know why I'm so embarrassed, it's not as if Amelia hasn't already seen it happen in public. But I think it's more than that. It's the shame of having forgotten for however long or short a time that Ruby existed. That Nick existed. That they both died and have been gone from me for these four months. And that I forgot them so easily.

When I drive past the gatehouse, I think I see a light in the top window, but then the sun rises and the panes of glass all reflect its brilliance; I think nothing more of it. Back at the manor, all's quiet, like the house is waiting for me. Like it knows it did something wrong and doesn't want to frighten me away. Knows I'm a flight risk, despite the hook in me of the memory of Ruby calling 'Mummy', and it's on its best behaviour. That little voice that can't exist. That I must have imagined. That woke me just in time. I sit in the car for a full five minutes, staring at the house, arguing with myself.

You should go. Get your stuff and go. Head back to London, or anywhere at all. Book into a hotel. It's not like you can't afford it. Call Albert, he'll arrange it.

But part of me suspects Albert Lowen won't, or he'll argue with me at the very least. Tell me I should stay. That this is good for me. That I'm imagining things because of the grief – *It's part of the process, trust the process.* Shut up, Albert.

I stare at my engagement ring for a bit, run a finger over its facets, feel the chill, then get out of the car and head for the front door.

9

By midday I've written precisely five hundred words, and deleted four hundred and fifty of them, so I decide it's time to go for a walk. I don't want to run into anyone today so I avoid the village, instead heading into the woods behind the house. Amelia's sent a couple of texts, which I've answered, thanking her and Carrie for their hospitality – as much to genuinely show gratitude as to ensure they don't appear on my doorstep for a welfare check.

The woodland isn't especially deep and dark – not ancient forest. There's a clear trail that boots and paws have beaten smooth, the trees are a tidy distance apart, as if planted by a designer with an eye for the open plan, and plenty of sun comes through the leaves above to light the way. There are no corners, nothing hidden, no undergrowth to conceal any what-have-yous of nature. Up ahead, there's running water and that's the way I go.

In a clearing, a wide pond is fed by a stream. On the opposite bank: a battery of late-season bluebells. What did my father say? Hear one ring and the Devil takes your soul? Or was it the fairies? I shake my head at the involuntary thought. I'm suddenly tired, and kneel, watching the reflections of clouds scudding across the sky, of branches swaying, of my own face floating there and I start to cry. Again.

I've done my best to lock it all up, but last night's weeping seems to have broken the dam. I keep crying, watching the surface fracture in small ways as my tears feed it, sending ripples out and out and out, like echoes. There's a stink on the breeze, overcooked meat.

In the liquid mirror, something appears behind my shoulder. Red and black and looming and a heat radiating down at me. For a moment I think it's the corn dolly come for revenge, that I let them burn her yet again. I scream, lose my balance and fall forwards, hands out, splashing up to my elbows in the water, mud between my fingers, and then the image is gone. I look over my shoulder, whipping my head around, trying to find whatever it was, but there's nothing there.

Mummy.

Across the pond, in the middle of the bluebells is a child. Solid and real. The pink dress my daughter wore the day Nick strapped her into the car seat and didn't bring her home; the white stuffed rabbit that went everywhere with her and burned as surely as she did. But I can't see Ruby's face, it's like the air in front of her is fogged or smeared like dirty glass. She begins to fade, becomes a white mist.

Mummy.

Then she's gone.

My daughter's gone and I run back to the house faster than I knew I could move, don't stop until I'm at the kitchen door, when the strength goes out of me and I fold to my knees and throw up the little that's in my stomach.

~~~

I dig the phone from the zipped section of my laptop bag, where it's been for a very long time. An ancient Nokia 3310, guaranteed to make it through at least three apocalypses and be useable by the cockroaches that survive the nuclear war, should they develop hands with opposable thumbs. The charger's there too, and I have to plug the damned thing in; a watched battery never reaches FULL so I go and make myself another coffee with the fancy machine, take the laptop out into the garden and tap another chapter that I suspect won't survive the first edit. My heart's not in it and nor is my mind. My patience lasts an hour before I head back inside, find the battery at 80 per cent, and it's back out into the garden, praying the old SIM still remembers its stuff.

Thumbing through the Contacts doesn't take long – back then, I didn't know anyone except a selection of police officers, counsellors, child protection officers and a few psychiatrists who I never saw more than once.

Hammett.

Gus Hammett.
~~~

What if he's changed his number, changed his phone? Be serious, he's the generation that hangs on to their phones forever. But what if he lost his, lost the SIM, damaged it? What if he's died? No one would have thought to tell me, not after all this time. No one would have known where to find me and that was the whole point. I hit CALL after a mere five-minute procrastination.

'Hello? Polly?' He answers on the first ring. Uses that name, not the one I'm now known by, nor the one I write under. The name – the old name, the one I left behind – is an electric shock delivered via the ears. It rattles my brain and shudders through the rest of me. 'Oh. Don't call me that.'

'Sorry, sorry. I forgot. It's been so long.' He clears his throat. He sounds old. Well, older. 'It's Everly now, yes?'

'Yes.'

He doesn't say *How are you?* like an idiot but rather *What happened?* Because he knows if I'm calling after all these years, something happened. I tell him. I tell him everything and he's silent, no noises of sympathy or assurances it'll be alright because God or whoever has a plan – all things I heard back then and again recently from the majority of people who dealt with me. At the end of it, he just says *Everly* and I can picture like he was back then, just saying *Polly*.

He was mid-fifties then, must be mid-seventies now. And the voice when he finally says 'You should have called me' is at odds with my memory of him in his office, sitting behind the brown desk while I huddled on the couch on the other side of the room, because he was smart enough not to approach a traumatised thirteen-year-old. *Older, Ev,* I tell myself, *he's older.*

'I'm calling you now.'

'OK. OK, why are you calling me now?' The tone strikes a familiar chord, warm, empathetic, no nonsense – the thing that always set him apart from everyone else I met back then. He never treated me as a curiosity; never picked at what I'd survived. What I'd done to do so.

Plenty of thirteen-year-olds are murderers. But not many under my circumstances. Not all do it to survive. Not all do it to their father. Not all had a father like mine.

'I think... I think I'm going mad.' I take a deep breath. 'Because if I'm not, then the stuff my father talked about – raved about – might be true.'

The bell over the door rings loudly when I enter; 'The First Apple' is painted in gold on the shop window. Another sign, neatly lettered, offers tarot readings, aura cleansings and cream teas. The space is jam-packed with candles and incense and crystals, potions and powders, a variety of floral and herbal infusions, statuettes of various goddesses, the occasional horned god, wands plain or crystal-tipped and wrapped with silver and copper and gold. One wall's taken up with a very full bookshelf: Wicca, yoga, religions of the world, histories of witchcraft, the entire Worst Witch series, compendiums of lore and legend, recipe books, guides to alternative medicine, several editions of *Culpeper's Complete Herbal*, and beginners guides to magic. Three racks of clothing – dresses, cloaks, shirts, trousers, embroidered jackets, everything made of velvet and silk – take up one corner. It's a *very* small area, *very* full. A stack of greeting cards for various occasions, a pyramid of chocolate next to one of rock candy, and an old-fashioned cash register lay claim to the front counter.

Gus Hammett sent me here after I spoke to him this morning, although it wasn't his idea.

Actually, he told me to leave. That I should get out of the house, out of the area, back to London and as far away as I could. Go anywhere else. Talked about evidence and proof, about investigations and dangerous situations.

'But I don't feel afraid of her.'

'Doesn't matter. You say she's warned you twice? That says there's something to be afraid of.'

I don't say to him how summer arrived, and I didn't care. How I'd dream, sometimes, that they'd come back: that I'm singing and Nick's out in the garden, turning the tiny patch of earth that was ours, chiming in on choruses or making up rude lyrics. That the little one's in her bouncer, giggling, and I pick her up, carry her outside to watch her father, digging and sweating. Then we're all laughing, and he comes over to me and wraps us in his arms and it's so warm and safe and it's summer right there – until it's not. Until I wake up and they're both gone again. And now I'm in this house that's only ever held me, one they never knew, never breathed in, never sang or laughed in. Yet my daughter's here. Or something with her voice. I don't tell him that sometimes at night I just embrace the dreadful cold of this place because it's the closest I can get to death. At night when it feels like the darkness of the grave, I throw back the blankets and let the chill creep into me until it feels like ice in my very bones. It's the closest I can get to them. The closest I can follow where they're gone from me, deep in the dirt. In this cold house that's the last refuge left to me when it's all gone so very wrong.

I just said, 'But what if she's here? What if my daughter's here? I can't leave. Not until I know... Until I have proof.'

'Everly, I'll come and get you. Tell me where you are.'

But something wouldn't let me say. The thought that he might drag me away in a straitjacket before I can find out what's going on. If it's Ruby or... something else. I thanked him, promised I'd be careful and then hung up. Turned the phone off and stuffed it back into the depths of the laptop bag.

Now in this fragrant shop, I'm filled with doubts; fairly sure I'm an idiot. That my solution is madness or a sign of it. I'm almost about to leave when soft words reach me. 'Hello, my lovely, what can I do for you?'

A head pops up from the wispy curtain behind the counter.

'Oh. Hello. Amphillis, yes? Amphillis Caston.' Remembering Ameila's warning, I'm careful not to call her 'Phillis'.

She laughs. 'For my sins.'

'Get enough custom here on the island?'

'Tourists are good for souvenirs and trinkets. Locals are good for proper craft. A hedgewitch is never out of work.' She looks me up and down, narrows her eyes. 'What are you after? Didn't I see you with the vicar and her wife?'

I nod. 'I'm Everly. Amelia and Carrie were kind enough to take me along to the straw witch's... celebration.'

'Ritual is the right word, I think.' She shrugs. 'Though people get a bit funny about that one. What can I do for you?'

'How do I... summon someone? Thing?'

'You don't.' She squints hard at me. 'Where are you staying...?'

'In the big house along Martham Road.'

'Morningthorpe Manor?'

'Yes, I guess. Just for a bit of... respite.'

'Could have picked a better spot. Somewhere more, well, restful.' Her lips have pulled into a thin line, as if she doesn't trust me. 'If you're staying there? You're the wrong sort. Whatever's after you is coming no matter what and you deserve it.'

'But—'

She shakes her head. 'I'll have no truck with them who live in the cold house, nor aid them. Take my advice, it's free: get the fuck out of there. Get out of there, and out of here.' She looks angry and afraid, and I'd ask more questions, about her echoing of my phrase *the cold house*, but she's come around the counter and is herding me, so much like a sheepdog I wonder if she'll nip. Before I can beg her patience, she's got me out the door, which closes firmly behind me, the lock snapping with finality.

10

I'm surprised when it's Carrie who answers my knock at the vicarage.

'Hello! How's the head?' Her smile's so bright I hate her a little bit.

'A bit murky this morning but I had painkillers and a lot of water. So: better. How about you?'

She groans. 'A reminder that I'm not as young as I think I am. Do you want to come in? Amelia's not here – duties on the mainland.'

'I thought you'd be in Cambridge—'

'No classes this week.'

'—but you're probably the one I need to talk to, actually, since you seem to be a repository of local info.' She leads me into the lounge, and I try to repress the memory of my tears here, the way my heart felt torn from its own betrayal. I sit on the couch, and she takes the armchair across from me.

'Well, I sort of collect that wherever I go. A compulsion, really, a bit like bringing home pretty rocks. Oh, tea?'

'No. Thank you. I wanted to ask you about the place

I'm staying. Morningthorpe Manor.' It occurs to me that if Albert had called it 'a manor' when he told me about it, I might have twigged it was something larger than a two-up, two-down, but he did not. In fact, the name 'Morningthorpe Manor' didn't appear anywhere on the map, at all.

'OK.' Carrie sits back in her chair, wriggles into the cushion. 'I know a few things. What do you need?'

'Well, how old is it? Who owns it? What bad things happened there?'

'You mean, is it haunted?'

I nod, don't mention the ghost I might have brought with me. Surely brought with me even though there was no sign of Ruby in the home she began in, the only place she'd ever lived. I don't mention it because that would definitely be a sign of madness.

Carrie pinches her bottom lip, pulls on it, thinking. 'The current building's been there about two hundred years. Before that there was a priory, right up until Henry VIII's Dissolution of the Monasteries. The land was awarded to a family that had done Henry some service or other – no records as to what it specifically was, so you can bet it was probably awful. The Morningthorpes converted the priory into a house and lived there for about a century, give or take.'

'Then?'

'Mysterious fire. Rumour has it the locals were not fond of the family, hoped to get rid of them via a barbeque – a popular method in this area, you'll note – and they did burn, the Morningthorpes, in about 1820 buuuut the estate went to another branch of the family. A niece, who took on the name and built a new mansion in 1824, moved in. Kept a much lower profile apart from the occasional charitable venture, like funding a renovation for the village hall.'

'Not the church, though?'

'Well, it was still functional back then and the new improved Morningthorpes had a pew in there and all. But it's fallen into disrepair over the last century and the Morningthorpes seem to have fallen into agnosticism? Or apathy? At any rate, a distinct lack of a desire to fund the church. Amelia says the dioceses keeps trying to sell it off, but no one wants it. I mean, you've seen it. Would you buy it?'

'I can't see even the most rabid renovator taking that on.'

'Nor me.' She sits forwards now, elbows on knees, fingers steepling. 'Do you know them? The Morningthorpes? Is that why you're staying there? I mean, I didn't want to pry...'

'Never met them. It was all organised by a lawyer. They're away, I needed a place to stay.'

She grunts. 'Didn't realise they weren't home. Then again, why would they tell me? Or anyone for that matter?'

'But nothing's happened there? Apart from a fire a very long time ago?'

Carrie looks as if she's weighing up her next words. 'The old structure, the priory? They called it "the cold house". It was where witches were dealt with after their trials, those found guilty. There was a well, apparently, down in the root cellar – supposedly they threw the women in. Unusual, given the traditions of burning, drowning and hanging, but I suppose throwing someone down a purportedly bottomless pit is equally lethal.'

I think about waking up with one foot hanging over that abyss. Mummy. I can tell from Carrie's expression she already thinks my line of questioning is weird. 'Right. Thanks for that. Good to know.'

'Are you alright there? On your own?'

'Fine, never better. Solitude's great for a writer, getting words down.' I pause. 'And Amphillis Caston? Not a big fan of the Morningthorpes?'

'Not of the house at any rate. Makes sense: self-proclaimed hedgewitch, location where other such women were killed...'

'Right. Right.' And I make my excuses and leave.

It's my seventh day in the mansion when I wake to voices.

Not that little voice that sometimes sings to me from around corners or calls at night; the wisp of white I follow through corridors and into empty rooms, always gone when I arrive. I've not found myself back in the cellar, at least, and there's no sign of the key having returned to the lock, no temptation to simply turn it in the dead of night without any idea of what I'm doing. No finding myself balancing precariously, toes gripping prehensile. Mind you, during the days I pour words onto the screen. Some of them even stick; I almost hit the halfway point yesterday. So many words. A ridiculous number of words. A possessed, write-like-the-wind number of words.

I haven't seen or spoken to anyone in the few days since I visited Amphillis and Carrie, though I've answered Amelia's texts. Have ignored Albert Lowen's calls and texts and voicemails – haven't read or listened to a single one.

Now though: voices in the kitchen. Not the soft one whispering *Mummy, Mummy. Mummy, be careful.*

No. Voices, plural. Male and female, definitely adults, different volumes and modulations, ringing with the confidence of belonging *here*. Noisy burglars?

I roll out of bed, grab my cardigan, pad barefoot to the door, leave my room and make my way along the corridor to the staircase. The voices grow dimmer – they're moving away from me, away from the foyer. I'm quick and quiet as I descend. In the foyer, the front door is ajar, sunshine rushing in, a pile of luggage in the centre of the space, a pyramid of expensive matching green and tan leather suitcases, various sizes and purposes.

Burglars who make themselves at home...

I don't think I'm in any great danger, so I head towards the kitchen where there's the rumble of conversation, then something breaking, some well-bred swearing, the *shh-shh* of sweeping. I hang in the doorway and watch.

A man and a woman, late fifties, tanned in Spanish holiday style, dressed casually, he in cream shorts and a pink polo shirt, she in a pale blue shirt dress (both seemingly immune to the chill of the house). Neatly coiffed hair, the pair of them black turning to iron-grey. Seeing them, I think I'm safe in assuming that these are indeed Albert Lowen's clients, the Morningthorpes, returned early from their holiday. I'm glad I've kept the kitchen clean – always a temptation when you're on your own to let things pile up and up and up.

I could speak but I'm not quite sure how to say 'Sorry I'm in your house, there appears to have been some sort of a mix-up'. It takes a moment for them to notice me – in my T-shirt, shorty pyjama bottoms and oversized cardy, bird's nest hair – but the man does first, staring. Eventually he taps his wife on the shoulder, grinning hesitantly. The woman, clearing up the broken cup, turns with an irritated expression, spots me. Her expression flattens, blank, then she breaks into an Olympic standard smile.

'Oh, hello! You must be Everly! Albert's told us so much about you!'

'Has he?' *Why?* 'He has?'

'We're so happy to meet you at last! We've been wondering about you, hoping and praying to meet you. Without Nicky—'

'Nicky? Who's Nicky? Look, I don't think I am who you think I—'

'Nicholas. Nicky. Nick Morningthorpe. Our son. Your husband.'

'What?' I'm feeling spectacularly stupid, as if my brain's gone on holiday and left me behind.

'We're his parents, darling. I'm Iris, this is Harry. Your in-laws.' Her smile widens, shows even more teeth. 'We're family.'

~~~

I've been packing for what feels like hours.

The truth is I haven't been packing my bags at all. I've been sitting on the edge of the bed, staring at the suitcase I got out of the cupboard when I first stormed back into this bedroom. I'm torn. I'm torn between not wanting to leave that little voice – *Mummy*, the chance of hearing it again, *her* again, of seeing her, finding her – and the urge to get the fuck out of here. Out of this fucking cold house with its strangeness and all its unanswered questions.

Then again: here are my husband's parents. Purportedly dead. But not so much it seems, with their educated tones and Costa del Sun tans, and wide-open arms begging a hug as if they know me. As if this is a *home* for me to return to like a prodigal.

And I think about all the answers they might have. That Albert Lowen knew who they were. That he was
~~~

in contact with Nick. And he was in contact with Nick's parents. That Nick Morningthorpe had become Nick Mitchell when he ran away from home. And as much as I'd like to run, I need answers.

Just as I come to that conclusion, there's a tentative knock at the door.

Grief is a cave into which all must descend, while light is unthinkable.

The Anchoress of Rungholt, 1360 A.D.
[Before the Great Drowning]

11

'I told Harry I should talk to you first. Mother to mother.' She pauses, still in the doorway as if afraid of trespassing. 'Bereaved mother to bereaved mother, really.'

And I remember that she's lost her son as surely as I'd lost my daughter.

'I'm sorry for my reaction,' I say (although I'm not sure I am), waving her in. She crosses the carpet quickly, alights on the mattress next to me. 'I just... on top of the accident, the loss, there are all these secrets coming out. I feel like every time I turn around another one hits me in the face. Nick told me you were dead.'

She looks hurt, but also snorts a sort of a bitter laugh. 'I suppose some days he wished we were. I... I thought we were concerned parents, worried about his future when he seemed so cavalier about it. It turns out we were in fact very controlling parents. I can admit that now – have done so for the last ten or fifteen years when we didn't know where he was.' Iris covers her mouth with her hand; a diamond engagement ring even bigger than mine, a thick wedding band beside it, gleaming.

I'm suddenly aware of the chill weight on my finger that I'd thought I'd got used to. 'And I can admit that if we'd found him in those early days? I don't know if we'd have been any better. We'd just have tried to get him back – insisted as we had his whole life.' She shakes her head. 'We forced him away by trying to tether him to us. And now he's gone. Properly gone.'

She begins to sob and, awkwardly, I put my arm around her shoulders. 'I'm sorry.'

'You just don't think, when you're angry, that you're not going to see someone again. That you won't get a chance to apologise.' She cries, I notice, very prettily; in an ordered fashion. Very much unlike me. There are tears, delicately and perfectly formed, but no snot, no spittle on the chin.

'We generally don't get a warning, no.' I think about my family, my *birth* family. There were signs with my father – but none of us knew enough to know of what – and definitely no warning. Not that *that* day would be any different or worse than those preceding it, all those days that had run into years. My mother? Might she have known better? As an adult? Might she have fought if she wasn't so fucking passive and obedient? Beaten down by childbearing and beration? No warning until it was too late.

Iris pulls herself together with a visible effort. 'Everly, you owe us nothing, but we owe you – I believe you made Nick happy. You gave him a safe place and a happy home, and we're so grateful for that. Would you... would you stay? Just for a few days? Talk with us, tell us about your lives? Just for a little while so we might feel like we know our son again. Albert said you and Nick were together thirteen years?'

The mention of Lowen sends a spike of irritation through me; his lies, his plotting and manipulation. But that's not this woman's fault, is it? I nod. 'Thirteen years. Yes. A few days, Iris. Sure, I can stay. Just a few.'

She gives me a hug so hard that the air presses out of my lungs. Then she stands, smiles down, and reaches towards me. Her fingers touch the locket and it's like an electric shock. I jerk backwards, left hand going to the necklace. What I notice, among everything else, is her gaze flicking to my engagement ring; the naked hostility.

Then she's laughing again, shaking her own hand, and saying. 'Static electricity! I was going to compliment you on that lovely pendant.'

And she's at the door with the speed of a much younger person, the spring in the step of someone getting what they wanted. 'Harry will be delighted. Oh, and please don't be too angry with dear Albert – he's a very old friend. He thought he was doing the right thing, bringing us together.'

I nod; I'll deal with dear Albert later. As the door's closing, before I can stop myself, I say: 'Iris? Do you ever hear things? See things? Here?'

She gives me a tender glance, a little pitying. 'It's an

old house, Everly. Built on top of an even older one. There are echoes and noises and shadows without source. Such places have a strangeness about them. Sometimes I think I hear voices, crying, but nothing's there. Just my imagination – the atmosphere lends itself to that. We'll see you in a few hours, yes? That's enough time for you to tidy up? Do you have a pretty dress? Nola will have lunch on the table at midday, sharp.'

And the door is closed before I can ask who Nola is.

A little past 11 a.m., I manage to sneak outside for a breath of fresh air, because sitting in the bedroom like a sulky teenager who's been told to wear something pretty isn't helping.

At first, I head towards the path leading to the pond and the bluebells, then I think about the smell of burned meat, the seared thing behind me, and detour towards the front gates, my sneakers *crunch-crunching* on the gravel. The little gatehouse stands silent and waiting. I wonder if Nick ever stayed here when he was arguing with his parents, when he simply couldn't bear to be under the same roof. Was it a refuge?

Iris had certainly taken the blame for the estrangement, yet there were no specific details. She'd *said* the blame was theirs. I find myself wondering what her seeming openness, her generosity with guilt, was designed to hide. I might be imagining things; Nick never complained about his parents, never spoke of them either good or bad, merely said they were dead.

I peek in the windows of the gatehouse. Is there a key in the manor? How long since anyone's been in there? The curtains are pulled back, some of the sunlight has seeped through its mucky windows; there's the edge of a carpet, the shadow-shapes of furnishings. A sitting room, I think. Deeper in the room, a misty form darts past the doorway, along the corridor maybe. I blink; did I imagine it? Am I just imagining everything lately?

It comes again, back the other way, same speed. Small, quick and white.

I try the door. Locked. The windows also don't shift. I walk around the building, find the back entrance equally unyielding. When I arrived that night, were the curtains open or closed? To be honest, I'd barely noticed the gatehouse itself, let alone the status of the soft furnishings. My phone beeps at me, breaking the silence and making me jump; that alarm I'd set to get back in time for lunch. Wouldn't want to be tardy.

~~~

There's something familiar about Nola but I can't quite put my finger on it, and I have to stop myself from staring at her as if trying to pick her out of an ID parade. The lunch is delicious so I can give that my full attention. Maybe the housekeeper, for that's what she seems to be, just looks like a generic grandmother – not an old one, no.
~~~

Or not spectacularly so. But a little older than Iris. Face blank, eyes too; automated. Maybe that's the expression of long-term domestic staff; Stockholm syndrome.

Harry's sat at the head of the table, Iris to his left, and me to his right. I've not set foot in the formal dining room before – not much point. A walnut banqueting table for fifty, an ornate pink marble fireplace (unlit), sideboards, portraits, statuettes and other pieces of art, a chandelier hanging over all like a sword. I catch the glance Iris gives my jeans and T-shirt before she rearranges her features. Another glimpse of that anger, quickly veiled.

'Hello, I'm Everly,' I say to my father-in-law as I shake his hand; it occurs to me I've not yet said a word to him.

'Pleased to meet you, Everly. I'm Harry Morningthorpe, and we're very happy you're here.' I think I see Nick in his features, more so than in Iris's face.

Despite Iris's earlier comment, I don't have to speak much at all. They don't ask me anything about their son, about our life together. Instead, lunchtime is filled with stories about *their* darling Nicky, their life together, how clever he was, how handsome and sweet, never a bother until the teenage years – isn't that always the way? – the holidays they took, how good his Spanish was, how very fond he was of Nola and she of him.

'And Nola went on holidays with you?' I ask as the woman departs taking empty plates with her. She's said not a word the entire time she was serving.

Iris nods. 'Every summer we close this house and go

to the one in Spain. Of course Nola comes with us, we'd be lost without her.' She gestures around. 'The place is too big, really, for just us – we thought we'd have more children, that there'd be grandchildren by now – but that wasn't to be. Yet we can hardly leave it, can we? Not with all the history here, the family legacy. There's a responsibility in that.'

Her voice trembles but she doesn't seem to acknowledge there *was* a grandchild. Or does she think she's being kind? Smoothing over my child's truncated existence?

'When did he run away?' I might be kinder but something's not ringing true about all this.

'Seventeen,' says Iris. 'Seventeen. When we were in Spain, he was supposed to be at school. By the time we returned home and realised what had happened... he'd left no trace.'

It takes a lot to leave a 'loving family' behind like that; takes a lot to leave a bad one too. And it takes a lot to disappear so completely that you can't be found. To stay beneath the radar when you start again. And Nick, so far as I know, didn't have government officials providing him with a new identity. A seventeen-year-old siphoning enough money out of the family fortune to buy a flat, build an investment portfolio. Impressive levels of scheming.

'What about your family, Everly?' Harry asks, sliding back into the conversation, perhaps as a diversionary tactic.

'I'm an orphan,' I say. Lie: 'Don't know anything about my birth parents. Was left on a church doorstep, as is the way of such things.'

'And you never felt a desire to find your people?' Harry sounds concerned – possibly at my lack of familial feeling.

'No. Orphanages raised me. A few kind people but a lot of unkind ones.' This is generally enough to shut down questions and it seems to work on Harry, but I suspect he'd like to ask more. I suppose he thinks tomorrow's another day. Tenting my serviette on the table, I push back my chair. 'If you'll forgive me, I need to go into the village.'

'Visiting friends?' asks Harry. Iris seems to have composed herself and is watching me.

'Ah, no. A visit to the chemist. Lady problems.'

As expected, my father-in-law turns pink and blusters a little, telling me to drive carefully. I ask Iris if she needs anything and she shakes her head.

As I go upstairs to retrieve my handbag, I realise what's been bothering me since I met them. Since I had my chat with Iris. It's an absence, a lacuna: neither of them has asked anything about Ruby. As if my daughter – Nick's – never existed.

I touch the locket, feel my own warmth diffused through the metal – the way jewellery should react – and I croon, *Hush, hush,* as if lulling a baby to sleep.

12

WELCOME TO THE WORLD

A birthing suite in an expensive private hospital I know we can't afford, and he tells me not to worry about it. That I'm worth it and so's our baby. That it's taken care of – he rightly thinks I'll forget about it after they pump me full of drugs so I don't feel it when Ruby's cut from me.

I almost died, they tell me later, blood loss and 'complications', but I've no memory of anything beyond the first labour pains, beyond my water breaking on the new leather sofa while we were watching TV and I was trying to forget that I was the size of a whale even though the belly in front of me almost obstructed the screen. The drive to the hospital, Nick being ever-so-gentle and kind and patient, and me being ever-so-awful because I feel like I'm coming apart at the seams and the only thing in my mind is the fact that my hips are going to be dislocated to let the baby out. What if mine don't work? Also: dislocated hips.

But, they tell me later, I should have died. They didn't know why I didn't. Because I definitely should have. They tell me so many times it's like they're aggrieved. That I've inconvenienced them by not meeting expectations. Not the first time I'd refused to die, I think about saying, but don't.

I've got six weeks ahead of me when I'm not allowed to do anything lest I pop my stitches, lest I become undone. To be honest, the whole experience, the nine months of a changing body, of giving birth, of the nightmares returning, feels like an absolute and comprehensive undoing. I don't love Ruby until a few weeks later, finally at home, she cries and I reach for her without thought and she looks at me like I'm the sun. It's not all smooth sailing, there are hard times, there's depression and a lowness in my spirit that I can barely get on top of some days. But eventually. Eventually, a new sort of rhythm is established and I keep writing in those moments when she sleeps, one word in front of the other until it's done.

And there are nights when Nick tucks her in to give me a break, and I listen to him telling her stories because I think he forgets the baby monitor is on. I heard him talking about his family, then, as if they're alive; talking about them in a way he never has to me. It's not a lot – just my mother said this and my dad said that – no names, no mention of places, but the happy snippets of memory you hope a kid can take with them. I don't mention it to him because it feels like I've eavesdropped on something private.

We're in a place that, for a while, feels right. Contentment and comfort. It took us a long time for me to get pregnant; I think we'd stopped expecting it. Nick's making good money (although not really private-birthing-suite good) and my

PhD's done. I don't have to make coffee for anyone for a while at least. There's breathing space and the book is done, my disguised terrors are on the page and the nightmares are gone as if exiled.

Shyly, I give it a title – as if naming it is the last step in claiming ownership – and contact an old PhD friend. A committed academic, she'd also published three novels. After a couple of patient breaths, she agrees to read it. I don't expect to hear anything back for months, if at all. It might, I'm all too aware, be terrible. It's a month when she calls: All the Hollow Bones *is brilliant, she says, and the agent she showed it to agrees. Would I be interested in signing with the agent? I am and I do. A publisher loves it too, but only enough for a one-book deal. It does well, that book by A.S. Valentine – my third name – well enough that the publisher would like another, but I know I don't have another story in me. I know that I fed the book with a deeply personal horror and it's been put away from me; it's dormant. If I start poking at it, what might happen? The publisher lets me go with a sigh, perhaps the way a mother wolf does with a pup she always suspected was too weak to survive. The agent tells me she'll wait – it's quite romantic, like a wartime romance – and checks in twice before disappearing.*

We are happy, Nick and I. We have Ruby. We have each other. We have just enough money in the bank against appliances dying, a plumbing emergency, possibly a brief holiday. There's a buffer. He likes his work, I'm happy at home for now. Sometimes he's short with me, sometimes the phone rings and there's a hang-up, sometimes he snatches at his mobile if I'm passing by, but I don't think on it.

We are, I believe, happy.

~~~

I retrieved the Nokia from the laptop bag before I headed to the car. The speaker function's given up the ghost so I wait until I'm once again sitting in the empty courtyard of Mabel's Café before I turn it on. Still plenty of charge and a bunch of missed calls. No messages.

'Lovely to see you again,' says Mabel as she puts my order on the table: a coffee I want (no matter how bad it might be) and a scone I don't but ordered to buy myself extra time and not be bothered. I make the call when she's gone inside. Reliable as ever he picks up immediately – I imagine him staring at the phone since I first rang. A sign of my self-absorption, to think he's got nothing better to do.

'Everly. Are you alright?'

'I need a favour, Gus. I assume you've still got contacts?'

A reluctant *Yes*.

'I need to know anything you can find about a couple called Iris and Harry Morningthorpe.'

'Like what?'

'Like anything, Gus. Good, bad or indifferent.' Trying my best to keep the impatience from my tone, I admit, 'Honestly, I don't know what I'm after. All I know is that something's not right.'
~~~

'Everly, you really need to leave that place. You can't be alone there.'

'Well, I'm not. Not alone. There are actual people here, not just a ghost.' *Or two.*

'I didn't save you all those years ago for you to throw your life away now.'

'You didn't save me,' I hiss, barely contain my rage. 'I saved myself. You just mopped up the aftermath.'

That anyone would claim to have saved me – even him – after no one paid attention to us *before*. When no one was watching or listening or noticing the bruises on my mother's arms and face because of who my father was. No one said anything when my siblings and I missed so much school because controlling our schedule, randomly, irrationally, was something our father loved to do, his position rendering everyone else *blind*.

'I did what I had to do to save myself.' I haven't felt so savage in years, not since the eve of my thirteenth birthday. Red washes over my eyes and I have to blink several times to unsee it. Trying to sound calmer, I add: 'Look at a firm of solicitors too: Higgins & Hyde. See what you can find out, anything that sets your old copper's senses a-tingling.'

He says my name again, my old one, my first one, and it's saturated with concern, with care. I hope my siblings heard that in my voice when I told them to hide in the cupboard. That no matter what came after, they remembered that I cared.

He corrects himself: 'Everly.'

'I'll be alright, Gus.'

'I'm worried you feel you've nothing to live for. That you're careless with yourself.' He speaks over a sob and I think I've blighted his life. That what he saw that day when he walked into the big old house in Surrey will never leave him.

'It's not that at all.' And I might be a little bit surprised to find I'm not lying. 'I don't feel there's nothing to live for. There's something to discover, something of mine I have to find again.' I clear my throat. 'Don't worry, OK? I'll take care. I'll call you tomorrow. Promise.'

And I hang up before he has a chance to argue with me, and switch the phone off.

I'm staring into space, weighing my options, when there's a flash of blue at the corner of my eye. Mabel's in the doorway, pulling on a blue jumper, asking if everything's OK, if there's anything wrong with the scone. The placement, the colour, bring back the memory.

'No, no. All good, thanks. Just had to make a call.' Splitting the scone and applying jam and cream, I take a bite so she can see how lovely it is. She goes back inside, smiling.

As I chew, I think not about her but about the woman who'd watched me that first day I was here with Amelia, the woman with the blue linen shirt and Nola's face. I wonder how she was in Spain and St Jude's at the very same time. And I wonder why her employers are lying to me.

13

I knock on the locked door of The First Apple until Amphillis Caston opens it. She did a valiant job of ignoring me for a good five minutes until it became clear that I'm more than capable of thumping until the glass cracks or I draw undue attention.

'What?' she snarls.

'I need to talk to you, *Phillis*. You don't know anything about me but let me assure you that I will put a brick through your window if the need arises.'

She glares for a long thirty seconds then curses, lets me in, locks the door again. I follow her past the counter, through the silky curtain into an overly warm kitchen decorated in earth tones. The oven's on, something baking. Smells like bread. She goes to a back door, grabbing up a lighter and case on the way, and I wonder if she's just walking me through to dump me out the other side. But no: it's a garden, overgrown, fragrant, the sound of bees buzzing in the riotous flower beds, two cats (one black, one tortie) who pause briefly in their climbing of a lemon tree in the middle of the yard to stare at us. A fountain with a mermaid on top sits off to one side, liquid pouring into a small pond mostly covered with water lilies. Carved wooden benches look to be extra smooth from use.

'Well?' she spins around to glare a bit more, before fishing a cigarette from the gold case and lighting it up.

'Those things'll kill you,' I say.

'You've got five seconds.'

'I don't know what – if anything – Amelia might have told you about me—'

'Nothing.' She says it too quickly for it to be true.

'Carrie, then.'

She looks away, mutters, 'I'd trust her before the other.'

'Right.' I close my eyes for a moment. Open them again. Maybe her expression's softened. I say, 'I lost my daughter. I'm in that house, yes, but not through any intention of my own. I don't know the Morningthorpes, not really – it's complicated – but I've been seeing... something.' I wave my hands uselessly. 'Someone. Hearing her call *Mummy*. I think it's my child. My Ruby. That's why I asked you about the summoning.' Suddenly I can't get enough air. 'I didn't know what else to do, and leaving's not an option. Not until I *know*.'

Amphillis Caston paces back and forth, taking drags on the ciggie and blowing smoke rings upwards. 'That house is not a good place to be. Not a good place to do any sort of ritual like that – a summoning opens doors that can be difficult to shut. It would be hard even to do a clearing – old things, strange things, unhappy things hang around. Grab hold.'

'Which brings me to my first question: the house. What do you know about it?'

She takes another deep drag, staring, considering; I feel like I'm getting weighed against a feather. At last, she gestures at one of the benches, takes the one opposite. For a moment there's just the sound of the fountain trickling, reminding me a little of the stream in the woods behind the manor.

'Remember the bonfire?'

'The straw witch.'

She nods. 'That girl? The straw dam? No harm in her, and only a little magic. Not the first and not the last to die that way, but the most public.'

'How do you know? Carrie said it was all very much lost to time and history.'

'Because she wasn't without family, that girl, no matter what they say. She had a child, and a mother and a sister, and they stayed out of sight, but she had a name and they kept it secret and they kept the truth of all that happened and passed it down.'

'To you?'

Another nod. 'To those who came before me. I'm a link in a chain. Now, the Morningthorpes.'

I raise an eyebrow.

'A lot of women burned, but also a lot were taken in secret to the priory and met their ends there. After the Dissolution when the place passed to the Morningthorpes – who were related to the Prior of St Jude's – they kept the tradition going with their own agenda. In the Burning Times it was easy to point a finger, make an accusation, watch a woman burn, but that was too public and the Morningthorpes liked to get something out of the deaths of others.' She pauses when the black cat lands in her lap, demanding pats. 'Women still disappeared into the priory even though the monks were gone, right up until the mysterious house fire.

'For months, no women went missing, no hedgewives or henwives disappeared into thin air. But just because the priory was gone, didn't mean the Morningthorpes were. Another one came, built again on the old site, bided her time. Made nice. By then the trials had stopped, but the disappearances started again. Women mostly, some men, people who didn't mean anything much to anyone, but *we* noticed. The covens noticed, those who stayed hidden kept track. We know that with every disappearance, some fine thing happened for the Morningthorpe family. Their holdings increased, honours were bestowed, great and fortuitous marriages were made. Over the years, it changed to contracts won, stock market windfalls, fortunes increased, promotions given. We've watched. We've seen.'

'Then why didn't you do something about them?'

'Don't think we didn't try. But they're protected by something else. Nothing we've ever been able to find out or break. Don't get me started on how many hexes have been attempted.'

'Bit of a risk, don't you think? Owning this sort of shop? Wearing your pentacle on your sleeve in a place where you say witches disappear?'

'Too high profile, me. Not some little witchling they can remove. I'm too visible.'

'Hope you're right,' I say, then my mouth goes dry at a thought. I swallow, lick my lips. 'What about their son, Nicholas? The one who disappeared?'

She frowns. 'That's a while ago. Seemed a nice enough lad, what I recall. But he was one of them – sooner or later, he'd have done as they did. You know the surname hasn't changed? Not in centuries, because even when a woman inherits her partner takes on the name.' She shakes her head. 'But that lad would have done whatever he was told, to keep their influence and position. What they buy, they buy with lives.'

And I think about my husband and how kind he was, how gentle. How he felt like home to me from the moment I met him. How he loved Ruby and was so attentive to her, never complaining about changing nappies or warming baby formula, or having to get up in the wee hours to get her back to sleep.

And then I think about all the lies he told, how he kept the truth of himself from me. The lies he told about this and other things. A little voice in the back of my head reminds me I did the same, and I remind it that

I *was* genuinely an orphan, but he didn't need to know the circumstances of that. He had a family, a living one. He had more money than he'd ever admitted to – did he think I was a gold digger? Wanting to keep his assets hidden in the event of a break-up? I'd never know. I'd only ever have suspicions and that ache of betrayal that he hadn't loved me as I'd loved him.

'What about his parents?'

'They don't come into town unless they can help it. The housekeeper does the shopping, runs the errands. They take off for holidays around the world, spend part of the year in Spain. *He* used to come to the pub for a while, but folk didn't like the attention he paid to their daughters. They used to have maids up there, young women, used to help Nola with the shopping, but they've not had one for a long while. High turnover.' She says this last ominously. I think again about the well in the cellar. How deep it might be. 'Sometimes they don't seem to make it back across the causeway – or not so anybody sees.'

'Right.'

'Any other questions?'

'Got anything protective I can take? Gun? Condom? Cricket bat? Incense won't do anything against people, no matter how bad they are – unless they've got a severe allergy to something. It'll only work on spirits, right?'

'Seems to me the ghost's the only non-threatening thing there. I'd say drive away.' She stares at me. 'But I know you won't.'

'Don't happen to have a gun handy?'

'No, but I can source a cricket bat.' Amphillis sighs. 'Look, the ghost seems to want to keep you safe. You don't need to summon it. And you never saw it before you came here, did you? Then it's yours, it followed you. As I said before, a summoning will open doors, drag something else through and believe me, you don't want that. One more thing?'

I raise a brow.

'Don't fucking call me Phillis again.'

~~~

It's about 6 p.m. as I'm driving over a small rise in Martham Road; I can see over the stone fence and into the estate. Though it's still light outside, beneath the close-grown old trees it's dim, which might be why I noticed a flash of light on the top floor, in the tiny peaked window of the gatehouse. Swiftly, I kill the engine. Park out on the main road, just a little walk away.

I punch in the security code and the gates slide open, blessedly silent.

The front door of the gatehouse is ajar, no lights on the ground floor despite the shadows, but from the threshold I see a glow spilling down from the next level. I slide into a small entry hall, cased openings left and right, a short corridor leading to the back, presumably a kitchen, and beside it a staircase leading up. A flash of white flitters at the top, small and indistinct. I catch my
~~~

breath, hold it. Finally let it out before I get dizzy.

Testing each step before putting my full weight on it. The flitting form dances back and back and back as I follow, to a door, again slightly ajar, a weak light pooling on the landing. On tiptoes, I sneak-sneak-sneak. For a moment, I'm in my old home, in that big dark house, tiptoeing through it trying to avoid my father, trying not to attract his attention now that the screaming has stopped and I know he'd found my siblings in that cupboard where I'd told them they'd be safe. Finally, they're quiet, like I told them to be. Careful to stay in the shadows, I peek in. Iris and Nola, bent over old trunks, pulling out items of men's clothing.

'He'll need these,' says Iris excitedly. 'He'll need these.'

14

Back in the car, my hands are shaking. Can't say why, it's not like I heard anything particularly sinister, just that Harry needs some specific clothing stored in the gatehouse – but I did see as I tiptoed back, in addition to the old trunks the women were going through, a couple of expensive-looking overnight bags in another of the spare rooms. In the same green and tan leather as that pyramid in the foyer the day they'd ostensibly returned from Spain.

And I can't help but think that they belong to Iris and Harry and Nola. That the three of them were hiding in the gatehouse ever since I arrived at the manor. That Nola was spying on me in the café. All of which begs the question: Why did they vacate their home? Or did they? Did they rush back from Spain? Or were they here all along? Tans can be faked very easily. And why did they choose today to make their presence known?

In spite of myself I blush at the idea of them watching me as I ran after or away from things that might not be there – did anyone follow me into the woods? Hear me shrieking? Did they see anything? Decide I'm a nutter? Did they sneak into the house when I was out, go through my things? Nothing ever appeared tampered with, nothing was missing.

I turn on the Nokia again, call Gus. This time it takes him a few moments to answer. 'Sorry, sorry. On the other line.'

I realise I don't know anything about him. About his life now. There was a wife, once, years ago, a child on the way. I wonder where they are. I hope he's not alone. I don't ask, though, because I can't bear any more sadness, mine or someone else's. 'Any news?'

'Nothing on Iris and Harry Morningthorpe. Very respectable. No title, though, which is interesting.'

'Titles attract attention,' I say absently. 'If you just read Mr and Mrs Harry Morningthorpe, you don't think "Owns a gigantic historical home and has pots of money." Easier to not to be noticed.'

'True. Your solicitor, however, is another matter.'

'Yes?'

'There's no record of an Albert Lowen with a current practising certificate. The firm, Higgins & Hyde, doesn't seem to have been in existence for the last two hundred years.'

I close my eyes. Yet Albert Lowen managed my husband's estate. He was very real, very solid when he put his business card into my hand. He co-signed documents, got money into my bank account. Wait. No, he didn't; he said there was money aplenty, that it would be available to me if I needed it before probate. That probate hadn't actually occurred yet. Said it would take 'a while'. How simple might it be to transfer money from anywhere else? And I've hardly spent anything since. The new car, arranged by Albert. Morningthorpe Manor, arranged by Albert. But if my husband hadn't left a note for him to be contacted in the event of his death, then how had he found us? Me?

'Everly? Everly?' Gus Hammett's sounding a little panicked. 'He's not there, is he?'

'No. No, it's OK. He's not here. He'll be skulking somewhere in London.'

'Hope you're right. Everly, you need to get out of there.'

'Soon. Soon, I promise. I need some answers. Tomorrow, I promise I'll leave.' Even if there wasn't that promise or threat or hint of Ruby? I need the laptop; it's got the book on it, it's the place I'm storing this terrible second life, and I haven't backed it up to the cloud. I need it. I need to finish it, to get everything that's happened *to* me *out* of me. Just like last time, it's the only way to get peace – otherwise everything awful stays inside. 'I'll call you tomorrow, Gus.'

And I hang up as he protests.

I start the engine, drive towards the gates. Note the flickering light is still on in the upper window as I pass by on my way to the manor.

My life's divided into two parts: things I try to remember and things I try not to. Much of my childhood's partitioned off. Even the good stuff, the little stuff, those tiny memories of joy because they were all contaminated by what happened.

Of the Before. If I think of my sisters and brothers in those times when *he* wasn't home, of us playing in the fields, scampering across the stream, lying on a hillside watching clouds. For a small while, a brief span, it's lovely – then it's washed away in a memory of red, of how I lost them. So, every joy contains a wound.

After: foster families. The government trying to hide who I was, whose daughter I'd been, what he'd done; preventing the tabloids from tracking me, publishing photos with the words 'Sole survivor' underneath, and me, all waif-like and hollow-eyed and utterly lost. There were a few of those before Gus personally threatened as many editors as he could. With no family, no community, I was cut adrift. No relatives to take me in. I was generally lucky in the foster homes, found kind enough people – but *they* weren't lucky because that first year I would, without fail, wake screaming in the night. Even the most compassionate would soon grow weary of interrupted sleep, of the effect it had on their own children.

It stopped – I stopped – eventually, but only after Gus talked his wife into taking me in because he couldn't forget me, couldn't forget what he'd walked into that day. They were childless, then, no one else to worry about, and he'd sit by my bed as I screamed and cried, hand me a glass of water, say 'Alright, then?' and when I'd nod, he'd leave me be. Drove me to therapy appointments, waited in reception, then took me home again and never asked what I'd talked about.

And then his wife got pregnant, at last, and she decided... she decided she was uncomfortable with me in the house. Because he'd told her what I'd done, hadn't he? Because most husbands can't keep that sort of secret from their wives; the soul-destroying knowledge of what a thirteen-year-old had to do to survive. With a child growing inside her, she became fearful – understandably. When I was sixteen, I went to another foster home; when I was seventeen, I began to make my own way in the world. I kept the old phone he gave me, though, checked in every so often at the start. But that trailed off. Life got in the way, and I didn't want to think about anyone or anything that reminded me of what went before.

'Hello, Everly.'

Startled, I give a little jump as I'm heading towards the stairs.

'Hello, Harry.' He's sitting in an armchair in the front parlour, can see me clearly so there's no point in pretending otherwise.

'Care to join me for a nightcap?'

'Haven't had dinner yet, Harry.'

'Ah. Then an aperitif perhaps?'

'Thank you. A whisky.'

We sit quietly, sipping our drinks. You never realise how long a minute is until you're passing it in silence with someone else. Harry's the one to break. 'So, Dr Everly Bainbridge.'

I look at him, waiting for a question, but he just repeats 'Dr Everly Bainbridge.' It occurs to me that he's nervous. I think about Amphillis Caston's comments, about people keeping their daughters away from him; I'm not his happy hunting ground. Wrong age group, too confident, too self-contained, a mother (or once-was). He can't impress me with the sort of talk that might turn the head of a teenager, and so he doesn't know what to say.

'How did you meet Iris?' It seems like I'm taking pity on him, but knowledge is power. Let's see what he shares.

'Iris?' He says his wife's name as if he can't quite recall who she is. I wonder how much he's had to drink; then his gaze focuses, he nods.

'In Spain. We were both younger then.' He grins but it doesn't quite take. 'My second marriage, her first.' He leans over, confidential. 'She was getting desperate, if you ask me, thought her time was running out.' A snigger. 'Almost. But we got him, didn't we. Our Nicky.'

His expression is one of fond regret and it's difficult to decipher. Fondness for his son, regret for his wife? A little of both each way?

'And you took her name, I think? Only someone I

was talking to in the village said the Morningthorpes had been on St Jude's Isle a very long time – but you're not from here?'

His face twists. 'No. And why not take her name, with everything attached to it?' He snorts. 'Pound signs. What else did I have? My first marriage cleaned me out. And then there was this woman, offering me everything if I got her up the duff.'

When did he start drinking today, or has he simply not stopped for some time?

'And Nick was an only child.'

'Only had one good shot in me, apparently.' He snorts, slaps at his groin. 'Ah well, it's a poor workman that blames his tools.' Laughs uproariously.

'I suppose the temptation is to spoil them when you've only got one.' Christ, I hope I wouldn't have done that with Ruby.

'Iris has... standards. Nicky and I often failed to meet them, but I think he took it far worse than I.' He shakes his head. 'Not her fault, really, it's the upbringing. Harder for her, trying to teach him the ways and he resisting every step. She might have been different—'

'Oh, you're back, Everly.' I'd not heard Iris come in. I'd wanted to ask Harry *What ways?* but that will have to wait. We both turn to take in Iris, poised in the doorway, her smile fixed in place by her words. No sign of Nola. 'Did you get what you needed?'

'Oh, yes.' I pull the little white bag with its mortar

and pestle logo from my quick dash just before I fronted Amphillis and made myself unpleasant. 'All set.'

'Lovely. Just in time. Nola will have dinner on the table in fifteen minutes.'

Nola really is a whizz, one moment she's rifling through steamer trunks, the next she's plating up meals.

'Thank you, Iris. I'll go tidy up.' And I rise and leave the room with considerable relief.

15

I spend most of those fifteen minutes throwing my possessions willy-nilly into my suitcase. The voice in my head says I should have done this before. That I should have driven away after the gatehouse. Should have left the laptop and lived with the mystery of the ghost, and all the awful things inside me. That the ghost, if Amphillis Caston is right, is mine anyway and would have followed me. That it manifested here because of *me*. But what if it didn't follow me? If I left this place, what if it stayed? How would I live knowing I'd left it – *her* – behind?

I put the laptop bag into the hard-shell suitcase, making sure the clothes pad it, then open one of the sash windows. This room's at the back of the house, only one floor up; I breathe a prayer to a god that I don't believe in, and toss the suitcase out. It doesn't make much of a noise as it lands on the lawn. I hesitate before I send the handbag after it – if I leave it here, I'll have to come back up.

Eat dinner, then sneak out: much easier to do without dragging luggage down a staircase. I run a hand through my hair before heading to the dining room. I wonder at two people rattling around in this big house, just them and a housekeeper, and they still insist on being served in a formal dining room. When there's not a third diner, do they sit at opposite ends of the long table like some filmic farce, with Nola traipsing up and down its length to pass the salt?

I'm half a minute late, the pair of them are huddled at one end awaiting my arrival. Did Nick sit like this, where I'm sitting now, in this cosy little triangle? Iris gives me a glance, notes I've not changed into something more uncomfortable, and haven't actually brushed my hair. Her expression spasms, trying to hide the irritation. I'd hate to think, if life had been different, of bringing Ruby to visit, of her being told not to run, to sit quietly like a good girl, children should be seen and not heard, don't make a mess of your pretty dress, darling, or grandmama will get upset. Of course, maybe Ruby *is* running around this house and grandmama doesn't know it.

Harry looks a little chastened, not glancing at me, but Iris paints a big smile over her disappointment. Has she torn a strip off him for speaking to me about her earlier? How much had she heard? Just as I get my backside on the padded seat, Nola arrives, carrying a silver tray: three bowls of pumpkin soup on it and a plate of crusty warm bread. It smells good and I realise how hungry I am. I might have had a scone, but there's been a lot of nervous energy burned in between.

'So, Albert's been telling us all about you, Everly.' Iris pours me a glass of wine; I thank her, make a mental note not to drink it, not on top of a whisky and not when I need to drive.

'Oh?' I take a spoonful of soup, swallow it. A little salty, some spice, unfamiliar, in it, but delicious.

'Yes. That you're an orphan.'

'I believe I mentioned that.'

'Except you didn't mention that Everly Bainbridge doesn't exist. I mean, there's a woman sitting in front of us, answering to that name but Albert's been very thorough in his researches – there's no birth record for a woman of your approximate age. There's a marriage certificate, university records, but no sign of you being born.' She laughs. 'Although clearly you were, didn't spring forth from an egg!'

I take another spoonful of soup, follow it with a bite of crusty bread. Buy myself a little time, wait for her to make her point.

'So, if Everly Bainbridge doesn't exist, who are you?'

'I had another name, once, it's true. Wasn't always an orphan. But my family...' I lick my lips, unwilling to give these people any part of my life. 'Something happened. I've been Everly Bainbridge longer than I was anyone else.'

'Did Nicky know? Were you honest with our son?' Her tone is harsh. As if I'd seduced her boy and lied to him – as if she hadn't driven him away well before I met him. As if he hadn't already rejected her.

I shake my head and feel off-balance. 'I never lied to him. I was an orphan. But he didn't ask how I became one and I never offered.' *Just like I'm not telling you.* I yawn without knowing it's coming. 'The story is mine. It's all I own in the world now.'

Where did that come from? Did I say it out loud? I try to lift my hand, put more soup in my mouth but I've no strength, or maybe it's no will. My thoughts must show on my face because Iris says, 'It's the soup, dear. In the booze is so passé and everyone expects it.'

In my mind, the words *No one expects the Spanish Inquisition* blare, and there's not much else going on in there.

Iris rises. 'Come along, Everly, there's a good girl. Not long now.'

And I am a good girl, so obedient, and I can't even think of a reason not to be, although I'm sure there must be one. Standing is a bit of a challenge and Iris snipes at her husband, 'Help her, Harry, for fuck's sake. Must you be so useless?'

'Do we have to do this?' he mutters half-heartedly.

'Harry.' All she says is his name but it's enough. He's out of his chair, hand at my elbow, helping steady me as I rise. Walking is hard, my legs feel rubbery, not mine, but my erstwhile father-in-law guides me out of the dining room, along the corridor and into the kitchen. Nola's standing at the door to the cellar; she turns something in the lock as we approach.

It's the key.

'You didn't think we'd only have one, did you?' Iris sneers.

The door swings open and the sound of the light switch being flicked is so, so loud. The way down is illuminated by a series of naked bulbs.

'Careful on the steps,' Harry says, tender as a father guiding his child; as if he's not leading me into grave danger. I'd like to swear at him, but I'm no longer my own anymore.

As we reach the bottom, something changes in the black ahead of me. Something flits, white and wispy, then it's gone so quickly I might have imagined it. Harry marches me towards the hole in the floor, the lightless abyss. While I'm standing on the edge, trying not to sway, Iris pulls the engagement ring from my finger and I don't have the strength to fight her. I just watch as it happens, until there's a scuff of shoe upon stone ahead of me.

Across the well, in the shadows of the cellar, a slender figure leans against one of the tall wine racks. A scratch and crack of a match being lit, and a cigarette tip flares as the flame meets it. The smell of cloves fills the closed air. Albert Lowen lounging in the dark, the flame showing his face as he stares at me, expression neutral.

'It's time for you to go, Everly. It's nothing personal, not really, but nothing's free in this life. Everything has a cost, and you're another form of currency.' Iris's voice is soft in my ear, but its edge is sharp enough, hard enough to cut. 'Albert tells me you've no friends left. No one's going to miss you.'

Her hand's in the small of my back, I can feel very distinctly the outline of palm and fingers, and then the shove, quick and inexorable. My feet can no longer be trusted, my balance is gone and I am very suddenly entirely awake. It's no longer just a bad dream and I'm falling, falling, falling into the endless black.

The question you must ask yourself is 'Did you fall or were you cast out?' Here, I believe, one finds the difference between a saint and a sinner.

Anonymous, *Commentaries on The Fall of Lucifer,* 1882 A.D.

16

I fall forever.

I can't tell if my eyes are closed or it's just that everything is so pitch black it doesn't matter if they're open or not. I fall for so long that I'm not sure I'm moving anymore. Shouldn't I be dead by now? When you fall for so long, shouldn't the fright of it kill you?

It's not the fall that kills you...

It's so black it reminds me of the hidey-hole under the stairs I waited in while my father finished slaughtering our family, listening to him shout and chant and pray to whatever he thought was going to reward him for the sacrifice. Singing his litany of names: Freya, Dark Annie, Morrigan, Badh, Macha, others I can no longer remember because I choose not to. I listen hard, certain for a moment that I never escaped, never grew up, that he's coming for me even now. I might believe it too except there's the rush of wind past my ears, and I think the shock of everything might be shunting whatever drug they gave me out of my system.

It's not the fall that kills you...

And now I'm grabbing handfuls, armfuls of air as

I go. Maybe I'm screaming, maybe I'm not, yet there's definitely a noise, loud and guttural, no ladylike squeal, but the scream of my soul trying to get out of my body, as if it might be light enough to fly, if only it can escape the meat sack that is me.

At some point, I hit. I hit something friable and sharp and hard that makes an enormous racket on my impact. I imagine my eyes as computer screens, blinking, blinking, until the light gets smaller and smaller until it fades out completely. My mind stops working before the pain really registers.

It's not the fall that kills you...

Here's what I know about Hell: you can hang over it for a very long time and not realise until you lose your grip and drop into it.

I'm lying on my back, staring up and somewhere, somewhere far above there's a tiny glimmer of light. The electric bulbs in the cellar. Too far away, though, to see if there are three heads or four staring down trying to trace my trajectory. Can't imagine anyone's waiting around to hear me go *splat*.

I swallow, begin moving one limb at a time to try and figure just how fucked I am. Because my life could only get worse if I survived and then lay here, paralysed. Death could take days, just me, immobile and alone with my thoughts. Professional torturers couldn't come up with a better – or worse – means of destroying someone. Of course, it's so fucking freezing it might be quite quick. The thing about being faced with death when you've been considering your own demise for so long? You're most likely to realise you don't want it at all.

Yet everything responds when I move it. I'm sore and I ache, but I can sit up in my crumbling, grinding nest of whatever, and nothing's broken. Miraculous. I can't see a thing. I reach up, find the warmth of the locket still around my throat. How am I not dead? I fumble for the smartphone in my jeans pocket: all I can feel is the smashed screen, the way it cuts my fingertips, the blood making them slip across the fractured glass. It's dead as the dodo. A thought, and my heart leaps: the pocket of my cardigan still bears a weight.

The Nokia turns on. No signal and only a little charge, but the torch works – me and a Nokia at the end of the world – and I shine the light around me.

I'm lying on a mound of bones.

Skulls, ribs, disarticulated spines, clavicles, hips, arm bones and legs, tiny tarsals and metatarsals, carpals and metacarpals. The remains of all those witches, real and imagined, of all those maids whose tenures were so brief. Shreds of clothing, pieces of jewellery shining in the weakening glow of this poor, battered phone.

Looking up, trying to stop myself from crying, I concentrate on finding a way home. A means of climbing out of the well. Of saving myself. Of going after Iris and Harry and good old Albert.

The light begins to weaken, shrink. I can't see anything beyond a few feet. No handhold, no vestigial staircase. Nothing. Is this all a hallucination? Is this actually the second before I hit? Have I actually fallen? I pinch myself hard on the cheek, feel the slither of blood onto the skin. Then the Nokia winks out. One apocalypse too many for its wee valiant heart. As the darkness presses in, I start to cry. I give up, at last. Why the hell should I keep fighting when the world has expended a lot of energy trying to shake me off it: why keep holding on?

And when I'm deep in the pity party, when I'm considering using one of the sharp broken bones to slit my wrists and hurry things along, that's when I realise I can see the wrist I've been pinching.

Mummy.

I look up.

Maybe ten metres away, a small girl, spectral white, a stuffed bunny in one hand, poised, staring at me. Lips not moving even when the word *Mummy* comes again. I blink. She's standing in the mouth of what looks like a tunnel.

I'm exhausted. I think about lying down, pretending not to hear, not to see. I think about concentrating on being dead, willing myself away.

But the little voice is insistent, and the locket is almost unbearably hot against my skin, vibrating.

Mummy, Mummy, Mummy.

A torment and a burden and a tease and a motivation. I crawl off the pile of bones, but I also grab a broken femur, its end sharp and savage looking. Just in case.

The light begins to dim as my daughter turns and moves down the tunnel.

I hurry to catch up.

~~~

She never lets me get close enough to touch her, to talk to her. When I call her name for the first few minutes, she doesn't turn around; a reliable Orpheus looking straight ahead lest she lose what she loves.

The air around me is so cold, radiating from the dirt and rock, from the walls. In some spots the ceiling lowers until I have to crawl on my hands and knees, fearing I'm being led astray. That if I try to back up I'll just find another wall behind me, surrounded, entombed, but the light ahead is steady, keeps going, and weary as I am, I follow.

Eventually, we come to a rough doorway, and I trip into a room with coffins lying in niches, and a single granite tomb. At the far end of the space is a set of square stone stairs. The ghost is halfway up them by the time I get through the breach in the rock face. Doesn't pause, just keeps rising. I stumble after her and it's such a long way up – like I'm returning from the centre of the earth – until I see splintered wooden beams above me,
~~~

manoeuvre carefully past them, and find myself, at last, in St Jude's Church. The altar cloth with its silver dots suddenly makes more sense; if I counted them, there'd be thirty. The ghost's at the door, which creaks open though she doesn't appear to touch it, and I rush to make it out before all her light is gone from this place which smells too strongly of grave dirt.

Out.

Out into the churchyard and the full moon's face shining down.

No sign of the child.

No sign of my Ruby.

But I'm alive.

I think I'm alive

I can breathe.

No one knows I'm still around.

I dredge up the last of my energy and head towards the road – towards the path that will lead me to the vicarage.

17

It's not the fall that kills you...

I sometimes wonder if you know something's wrong before it happens, but you ignore it because everything else is taking your attention and you just can't add one more thing to the clamouring noise. And, ignored, the bad thing comes closer and closer, screaming louder and louder but you're still ignoring it because everything else is just too much.

I was juggling a four-year-old, trying to write a second book, trying to keep the flat as clean as I could, trying to remember to brush my hair and teeth, pinch some pink into my cheeks, trying to cook meals and not waste money I thought we didn't have on takeaways. Trying to maintain a relationship with a husband who was growing distant. I knew it. I knew he wasn't *there* even before he *actually* wasn't there.

I ignored the hang-ups on the landline, the caller who, just once, said 'You don't deserve him', the new clothes, the new cologne, late nights, weekend trips away. Ignored how protective he became of his mobile, and how often it pinged when he forgot to turn the volume down. Ignored the faint lipstick smears on his collars where he'd been careless, and the stupid lies because he'd never been good at lying – concealing things, yes, lying, no.

At some point, one of us would have left.

Maybe him, but maybe me.

Harder for me to leave because I had Ruby and nowhere to go. The flat was his and I didn't know how much money was hidden away. And I don't know if he'd have let me take our daughter. Not that men want to care for their kids, but they want to own them; they go and get new girlfriends, new wives, then hand off the children to them like some sort of bridal gift. *Here's one I prepared earlier.* Add that uncertainty to why I chose to ignore the call of the bad thing.

At the funeral, there was a woman.

A redhead in her mid-twenties, a receptionist from his work. Crying like her heart was broken when I couldn't even muster a tear – not because I wasn't howling on the inside, but because nothing worked anymore. She didn't look at me, couldn't. I felt so tired, so old, but I also felt kind of sorry for her; I just thought how stupid she was, that she'd believed whatever he'd told her. That she thought he'd never get bored with her as he had with me. That, if he couldn't be faithful to one woman – the one who'd had his child – why would he be faithful to a different one? Sympathy notwithstanding, when I left I went over to her, leaned close, held her hand and said,

'Don't worry, you'll find someone else's husband. I'm sure there'll be a lot more in your future.'

I've wondered, on occasion, if he'd taken Ruby to meet her. If they'd gone to parks or restaurants where whatever-her-name-was played mummy, Nick road-testing her maternal instincts. I wonder if she was smart enough to pretend; if Ruby played to it, accepted it, acted as if one mummy is as good as another. It's a stupid thought and unfair; Ruby was four. But a mother's heart isn't a logical thing.

The point of all of this is that someone would have left.

Even without the fiery car crash, someone would have left.

There'd have been divorce, more or less messy, division of assets, sharing of child.

I wonder, now, if Nick might have planned something else – because in the event of a divorce, it seems to me that his secrets would have come out. Family, money, all of those things. Who he really was. So, maybe, Nick wouldn't have wanted a divorce. Maybe Nick – the Nicholas Morningthorpe that I didn't know existed – would have had a neater solution, one that didn't involve me learning the things I've learned. Maybe the man who'd plotted to disappear from his parents would have had other plots in mind. Given what his mother tried to do to me – did do to me – maybe this isn't so farfetched.

But in the end, he took my daughter from me anyway and left me to my own devices, and all those fractures made in childhood were opened and a worse person came out.

~~~

Unfortunately, or otherwise, the vicarage is dark. No one answers my knocking. There's no sound of anyone inside when I press my ear against the door. I stay there for a long while, trying to decide what to do. Glancing around, looking for the ghost girl, that flash of white in the darkness, but there's no sign. Her work's done, for the moment at least – maybe her work's done completely.

Do I try The First Apple? Will Amphillis let me in? Will she help or hinder? Here's the thing about asking for help: it leaves witnesses. And I don't want witnesses to this evening's work. I'm going to leave a red mess in Morningthorpe Manor. That'll teach them to throw me down a fucking well.

How long did it take me to get out of the Underworld? How long was I unconscious? How long did I fall? Maybe it's after midnight, maybe just before. Doesn't really matter.

I can walk. I've got a stabby femur. I've got the advantage of surprise.

What more could I need?

~~~

The gatehouse is abandoned when I arrive and slip through the estate gates, but I'm careful to stay beneath the thick woods that line the driveway, just in case someone's there, keeping watch. Just in case Nola with her beady little eyes is hanging around.

A few times, I think there's the flash of white darting between the tree trunks, but every time I look in that direction there's nothing. Either I'm imagining it or my daughter's playing hide-and-seek like we used to. I keep moving forwards, eking my way around to the back of the manor. I see my bags where I threw them; no one's been through my room yet, no one's gone looking for them. Or if they have, they don't think there's any hurry about retrieving them. They're so sure I'm gone, that no one's coming to look for me, that they've got all the time in the world.

Somewhere, not so far away, a fox screams, but it doesn't startle me. What's going to bother me now? After everything that's happened? I put the femur in a belt loop at the back of my jeans, head towards the kitchen door, find it unlocked, gently open it.

Nola's leaning over the sink, scrubbing at a pan, back to me, not paying attention to anything. I creep in behind her, and slip my arm around her throat, pull her up and apply pressure, while my free hand covers her mouth to keep any cries in, the nose to keep any air out. The femur's not for her. She struggles a lot, but she's got no purchase, not enough strength. I wait until she goes limp, then manhandle her to the cellar door – still unlocked. Again, what do they have to fear? No guests, me gone, no threat.

Nola doesn't wake as I drag her by her feet down the stairs into the crisp cold of the cellar, not caring when her head makes that *thud-thud-thud*. Nor does she wake when I tip her into the well.

There's a certain satisfaction in the act. A certain hollowness, too, but she spied on me, drugged me, watched while her employers walked me through the kitchen in my stupor. I owe her nothing.

Back up in the kitchen, I take a deep breath. Catch my reflection in the night glass of the windows: very pale, ghostly in fact, dirt on my face, eyes wide, lips far too red. I shake my head, force myself out of the bright lights and into the dim shadowy corridor. From the formal dining room, I can hear the murmur of conversation, the distance making it faint. Surely, they can't still be having dinner? Midnight snack?

As I'm passing the library, there's a sense of déjà vu when a match flares in the depths of the room, and a brief circle of light shows the face of Albert Lowen once more.

'There you are, Everly Bainbridge. My, but you must have some impressive angels and ministers of grace watching over you.'

18

I stride towards the lawyer, pulling the femur from my belt loop.

'Now, now. That won't work. Or rather it will, but it won't get you what you want.' He flicks on the banker's lamp, revealing his elegant perch on the edge of the large mahogany desk I've made mine, smoking calmly, suit immaculate, long thick hair kissing his collar.

'And how do you know what I want, you lying shit?' I draw back my arm, then strike. Lowen sways just a bit, and I miss, hitting instead the top of the desk, the jagged end of the bone gouging its way through the expensive wood. I gather for another swing.

'You can do that, or you can listen to me,' he says mildly. 'But keep your bloody voice down.'

This time he doesn't move enough, arrogant, and I catch the outer point of his left shoulder, feel the meat of him part, the jacket fabric rip, see the brief red well of blood. It stops very quickly. His free hand shoots out and grabs my wrist. 'Look, this is my favourite suit. Everly, just wait. Just listen.'

I keep pulling against his grip, trying to get away, but he's too strong.

'Fuck you!'

'I had a feeling,' he says, shaking his head. 'I just had a feeling about you, Everly Bainbridge, what a wonder you are. Throw you into a well and you just climb right out again.'

'Walk.'

'I stand corrected.'

'What if I hadn't survived?'

'Then you wouldn't have been the girl I thought you were.'

That gives me pause. I stop struggling. 'What do you want, Albert? I'm tired and I have some murder to do.'

'Everly Bainbridge, you were hard to find. Little Polly Waterbright that was.' I flinch at the name. The old name. 'So famous! So briefly, then *poof!* gone. All my resources, good and ill and I still couldn't locate you. Interesting that someone with your background should find Nick, of all people. Another one doing a runner.'

'You're not getting to your point. I'm assuming you have one?'

'I knew about your father – not personally, but what he tried to do, all the power he amassed with those deaths. It's talked about in places high and low. All those family murders. But he didn't finish, did he?'

I think about my father gasping as I drew the carving knife across his throat. I try not to think about that night, but I remember the determination that ran through me not to die. Not to scream like my mother and siblings.

He didn't expect me to fight back. He was used to being obeyed. He thought it was his due, all the power that would come with all that blood spilled from his own family. All the dark power that sits, unused, in me.

'A curious inheritance you took. Why do you think you didn't die in that fall?'

I consider, also, Ruby's birth, about being told I should have died. Confounding the doctors as to why I didn't.

'Are you the Devil? Are *you* what he was making a deal with?'

'A devil, not *The*.' He shrugs. 'A lot of outsourcing, nowadays, flattened corporate structures. But I am *a* devil, a personalised one, just not yours, nor your father's – your father, by the way, was bargaining with Dark Ladies far worse than little old me. I've been with the Morningthorpes, for my sins, since the seventeenth century. So, not your common or garden devil. More an executive-level devil.'

'What the fuck just happened, Albert Lowen? Because you brought me here and my in-laws threw me into a well.' I wave a finger at him. 'And before you spin me some bullshit, remember that I'm just about ready to start hitting you again.'

'That's the spirit!'

'Albert...'

'Your in-laws' family have been paying a tithe for a very long time. Lives and souls in return for favour, prosperity and power. They're Iscarites – you've seen the church?' I nod. 'They believe that without Judas Iscariot, Jesus wouldn't have become what he did. So, according to them, Judas did a little evil for a greater good.'

'That sounds like late-stage capitalism.'

'Accurate. My point is that bargains are made for things of value. Let's be honest, not all souls have the same merit, the same heft. Mothers for example are the heavy hitters. That urge to self-sacrifice! Fathers, not so much. Not all fathers, obviously, but a hefty percentage, and basically, they're very ordinary fodder. But a mother's soul?' He picks at his teeth, an unexpected coarseness. 'A weighty, sad, bright, brilliant thing. Do anything to save loved ones, especially children. Now that soul has a price above rubies.'

Ruby.

'Iris wanted something. *You* had a high value. *You* were her currency. Here's the thing: people either sacrifice themselves or are sacrificed – you're in the second category, no choice in it, really, and generally no time to object or think about it, and just say *No*. But you, my dear Everly Bainbridge, said *No* with your every fibre. Refusing to die under any circumstances. Magnificent. Honestly, you don't see a lot of that. I put it down to all that power you took from your father.'

'I didn't take—'

'You refused to die. You took his life. All the power he'd pooled in himself with the deaths of your family, those most precious souls? But he didn't get to complete his collection. You took everything he'd stolen. Yet you took it with no intent other than survival – you didn't want the power, didn't use the power. It's all just stored in you. All that potential. As a sacrifice, you're even more *puissant* – that's French.'

'How did you find me?'

'Newspaper articles and reports. There were photos of the grieving widow after the tragic and newsworthy car crash. I thought you looked familiar, then when I met you, I knew. Did a little digging, cost a pretty penny but you should feel flattered how much it took for someone to give you up. Don't judge too harshly – cost of living makes people do terrible things, I mean look at that financial advisor, frittering away all your inheritance before you came of age. In this case it was a records clerk, that's all, not even old enough to remember the case. They'd done a good job of hiding you because someone might have asked a lot of questions about why a member of the House of Lords had slaughtered his entire family, all except his eldest child, his favourite daughter, his little murderer.'

'The newspapers reported it as a house fire. Sole survivor.' I close my eyes, but the film of that night plays on the back of my lids, all tinted red. 'Let me go.'

'Are you going to stab me again?'

'Yes.'

'Then no.' His fingers tighten. 'Here's the thing: you not dying? It means your mother-in-law has not in fact fulfilled the terms of her agreement. So: things are up for renegotiation. And you are owed.'

'By whom? You'll understand I'm leery of making deals with a devil, executive or otherwise.'

'Fair. Owed by her. By them. By me – although I'm really just the facilitator.' He takes a deep drag on his cigarette, the tobacco blazing. 'Free shot. No obligations. Whatever you want, you get.'

'No cost? If it's too good to be true, it probably is.' My arm's going numb.

'No cost to *you*.' He pauses. 'A word of advice: be very specific in what you're asking for.'

I stare at him, know I shouldn't entertain such things, but I can't help myself. 'What did Iris want?'

'Well, all of this is about a mother's love. Isn't it?'

'Blaming the mother like every serial killer does – why not the Devil?'

'A devil. It's a classic for a reason. You and Ruby, Iris and Nick, Mary and her boy. Judas's mum and her darling child, hanging from a tree all weighed down by those thirty pieces of silver.' He waves a hand. 'A mother's love is the greatest force in the universe for good and evil. A thin line, easily twisted. Grief – grief does it every time. Too big and it poisons that love. Remember that Iris didn't sacrifice *herself*.' A grin, pleased with himself. 'So, Everly Bainbridge, what would *you* do to get your Ruby back?'

'Bit pointless, self-sacrifice, if I'm not able to collect,' I observe.

'Not my point. I'm saying that anyone can use another as currency.'

'Why are you doing this? Aren't you bound to the Morningthorpes?'

'Technically right up until the bargain failed.' Again, he shrugs. 'And to be honest, they're tiresome. The sixteenth century's a long time ago.'

I examine his expression; perhaps even a devil might be filled with contempt for those who commit awful deeds. I need more time to consider. 'Nick stayed in contact with you, didn't he? And his mother – the umbilical cord didn't stretch too far.' I say, 'Everything was a lie. You knew where he was, so did they.'

Lowen shakes his head. 'Actually no. When he left here, he did disappear. Never wanted anything to do with the family business. Seemed to have been socking money away for ages. Organised all his new documents, changed his name, slipped away into the night. Very clever. Very sneaky.' He holds up a finger. 'But he left instructions with his other lawyer, the one who only knew him as Nick Mitchell, to contact me in the event of his death. It was simple to talk said lawyer into handing over all the other matters – I can be very persuasive. Your husband wanted you looked after. And he wanted his parents to know what had happened to him. I don't think it was a happy childhood, but people find it hard to separate from family even in the worst of circumstances.'

'Did he know they'd do this? To me?'

'I don't believe so, but you can ask him yourself.'

'What? How? Oh, am I dead too? Is this hell?'

He lets me go; my arm falls nerveless at my side. 'No, no. Come along. And keep quiet, we don't want to attract any undue attention before we need to.'

19

We hang in the shadows of the corridor just outside the formal dining room, close enough to see in the door, far enough away to remain hidden. Lowen stands very close behind me as if he trusts me not to stab him again. I can smell a faint whiff of cloves and cologne and a strange chill comes off him; I can't but think that a devil should be like an inferno.

A figure bustles past us carrying a tray. Nola steps into the light of the room without a backwards glance. I swallow before whispering, 'I put her down the well.'

'Did you? Unfriendly. Lucky for you she's not made to take it personally.'

'Made?'

'From clay and bones and a few unpleasant things. Hard to have staff around the place that don't snoop and tattle. She's part of their deal, been in the family the last four hundred-odd years. Made her myself.' There's a note of pride in his tone. 'Now, look at the table. Who can you see?'

'Iris and Harry, there's someone to the left I can't quite make out, and... Oh God.'

'I know. Quite the sight, yes?'

I only know it's Nick from his posture, his height even though he's slumped in the chair, the width of his shoulders, and the single glossy curl on his forehead, black as a raven's wing. The only remaining bit of hair on his head, which is still more skin than he's got. Or rather, the skin and flesh are fused, an amalgam of crispy-looking black striped with fissures of dark red. The white cotton shirt (polo monogram over the chest) he's wearing is damp in patches where whatever is seeping from his burned body has soaked into the fabric. It looks like one of the shirts Iris and Nola had out of the steamer trunk not so long ago. *He'll need these*, Iris had said. *He'll need these.*

Now she's snapping at her only son, 'Sit up, straight, Nicholas.'

Lowen speaks low into my ear: 'He's alive – you were the price for that, Everly. Your life in exchange for their son returned. But, apart from her bounced cheque, so to speak, our Iris also wasn't very specific in her phrasing, so Nicky-boy's not the man he was.'

'Christ.'

'Nothing to do with it.'

'But if she didn't pay for her deal, why is he still there? I didn't die.'

'Well, Everly, here's the thing: you did. You just didn't stay that way. Bounced back like a rubber ball.'

'Or a bad cheque,' I say slowly. 'Then why—'

He looks impatient '—didn't everything revert? Because I felt it the moment you woke. Because I left things as they were and waited for your return. Because such moments require elucidation. Pontification, if you will. The chance to say "I told you so." And timing is everything.'

As if to make his point, Iris's voice sounds clarion-clear. 'We'll need another coin for bargaining. I'm sure Albert will renegotiate. That Phillis with the shop, with the tarot cards; she'd do perfectly well. Long time since we've been able to offer up a proper witch.'

'Iris, she'll be missed,' begins Harry but she talks over him.

'In the meantime, he needs to bathe in blood. It's an old remedy. That will give some relief, help the healing. Children would be best. You can arrange that.'

'No!' A familiar voice makes my heart sink. 'I won't.'

'Amelia Morningthorpe Willoughby, you will do as you're told.' Iris sounds like a martinet.

Oh, Vicar. What a mess.

'Aunty Iris, I'm not getting children for you to kill. Did you forget the rule about not drawing attention? You're neither liked nor trusted in the village; they only talk to me because I don't go by "Morningthorpe". Where do you think they'll look first if children go missing? I'll give you a hint – they won't look at the witch in the spook shop. Not when there's a monster in the manor.'

The sound of a slap.

'I know this,' Iris's tone a-tremble now as she tries to get her temper under control, 'is difficult. I know you've thought for a long time that you'd be the next heir, but–'

'I don't want to be the heir! I want no part of this. What you did to poor Everly. What you've done to poor Nick – he can't be happy about this. How can you think this is the right thing? Uncle Harry...'

'He's got no say in this! You think that worthless rake is going to take your side? I'm the source of all his luxuries and indulgences. Me! Not some penniless fucking vicar!'

Nick tries to say something. I can only tell because the fused lips move and there's a muffled mumble, no words distinguishable. His eyes are red jellied blobs in their sockets. I'm not sure he can see anything. There are no longer ears on the sides of his head, just seared stubs where they used to be.

Iris clears her throat, and I can hear the effort she's making to get her temper and tone under control. 'Everything I have done, I have done for this family. You will respect my decisions and you will not question me. There'll be orphans somewhere, Amelia, you won't have any trouble finding them, with that dog collar of yours and your holier-than-thous.'

In the shadows, Albert Lowen leans over my shoulder, fixes me with a stare and says, 'So, Dr Everly Bainbridge: what's it going to be?'

'I want my daughter back. Ruby as she was just before Nick put her in that car, restored to factory settings, nothing wrong with her. Not a monstrosity. I want to have a long and safe and happy future with my daughter. That's two wishes; two bodies and souls, yes?'

'Mrs and Mr Morningthorpe in return.' He nods solemnly. 'Come along, then.'

He gives me a gentle push and I stumble a little as we step into the room. The lack of dignity doesn't seem to matter as the sight of me is apparently electric. The four at the table look as if they've seen a ghost. Nola, powering down by the sideboard, doesn't appear to care one way or the other. Vicar Amelia looks guiltily horrified.

Iris is the first to speak, shooting to her feet: 'Albert! What is this?'

It seems I'm not even there. Maybe Iris doesn't bother talking to those she considers dead.

'Hello, Iris. Harry.' He gives the vicar a surly nod – 'Amelia' – turns his attention back to Iris and her husband. 'Here's the thing: you've not actually paid your debt. Your promised account. Everly, as you can clearly see, is not dead. She was the price for Nicky's return. You have therefore broken the vow and promise of the Iscarites for the first time since 1629. And so, Everly's made her own bargain with me which supersedes yours.'

'Albert, no!' Iris shouts, clearly thinking she can continue to order him around.

'Don't worry, Iris, no one's going to miss you,' I say.

'Albert, I demand—'

'Oh shut up, Iris.' His tone is only mildly contemptuous

as he raises his left hand and flames bloom upwards from the floor, like petals reaching before closing for the night. Iris and Harry are briefly blazing pillars, but they don't burn for long. Soon they're gone, drawn down through the polished wood, leaving nothing behind, not even piles of ash and bone. But I think I'll hear their final screams echoing for a while after.

Amelia's sitting frozen in her seat. Nick has turned to face me, and those gelatinous crimson eyes lock with mine, but I can't decipher his expression. He's too ruined. Albert wipes his palms together, as if cleaning them, then he gives me a sideways glance.

'There's another bargaining chip left, Everly.' He nods towards the vicar, and I think about how she'd befriended me all the while being part of this family. This sect. Then again, when she didn't know I was listening, she did seem to be fighting for her soul, a bitter action against her aunt. 'What do you say? Her for your husband? Him all brand new? Factory settings?'

And I look at my husband, and I think about the lies. I think about the redhead at his funeral. I think about him causing hurt to our daughter through carelessness and inattention. I look at him long and hard and I think I see begging somewhere in that wreck of a man, and I don't think it's for life. Because if he comes back he needs to answer to me; needs to explain his family. Needs to explain the woman at the funeral. All those phone calls. All those hang-ups.

And if I want him back? Wish him back? I have to sacrifice Amelia, and I'm not entirely sure she deserves that. She didn't push me down a well. Didn't kill my child. I shake my head. 'No, Albert. No. It's too much.'

'Fair enough.' And fire shoots from his hands once again and engulfs my husband because Nick was something that had not been paid for. He's repossessed goods.

'Now where's my—'

'Mummy!'

I turn to the corridor, to the shadows where we so recently skulked, and the white wisp of a child pelts from the darkness, getting more solid with each step, until she's wrapped around my knees and it takes all my energy to unpluck the grip and haul her up into my arms. And she's warm and soft and smells like mine, and all seems right with the world.

20

When an old Land Rover rolls up at the gates the next morning and Gus Hammett, who'd used the names Iris and Harry Morningthorpe to find their address, began banging on the intercom buzzer, we were already gone. But Amelia Willoughby answered, let him in. She'd made him tea, he later told me, and reassured him that I was safe. She promised him she'd get me to call him just as soon as I called her.

I wasn't quite ready to forgive her for not telling me who she was, but I did appreciate that she'd refused to obey her aunt at the end. Besides, who knew when I'd need the services of a fully fledged vicar who owed me several favours?

And I rang her after a couple of days, and she told me about Gus. By then I'd transferred the SIM – intact by the grace of something – into a new old Nokia 3310. I told him that I was fine. That I was safe. That I'd come and see him one day and buy him a whisky. And I would, when I figured out how to tell him I had my daughter back. How I'd got my daughter back. It's the sort of explanation that shouldn't be done hastily.

The flat is new, freshly built, no history in it, no trace of anyone else's lives to paint its walls. No echoes. Blank and possibly boring, but it feels safe. Oh, I know the land on which it's built has its own echoes and haunts, but the building itself is pristine. A big blank slate for us both.

Sometimes Ruby asks after her father.

Mostly she doesn't.

I wonder if, even young as she is, on some level she blames him. I'm not sure what she remembers, of the car, the crash, what came after. What it was like to be a ghost and why she came back when she did, where she did. One night I asked her, the why of it.

Because you needed me, Mummy.

Sometimes we play hide-and-seek, and she hides for so long I think she's gone for good. Just as my heart's about to break, she pops out from behind the sofa, or the wardrobe or the laundry basket, and her laughter washes all the pain away.

Albert Lowen drops by occasionally, though I've told him not to. Ruby likes him, thinks he's funny. He does magic tricks for her – except it's not a trick, is it? It's actual magic when he pulls a bird out of the air, or an egg from behind her ear, or that bloody puppy he produced from his briefcase that is only just getting the idea of toilet training. He returned the engagement ring to me, but I don't wear it; it's in a mismatched jewellery box in the back of my underwear drawer. I'll never give it to Ruby, but I might sell it one day – Albert assures me there's a healthy market for cursed trinkets.

Sometimes I let him in, he makes tea; sometimes I've bought biscuits. Sometimes he brings wine and we have a drink out on the balcony and talk until the moon rises or the sun sets. We talk about his history, and mine, everything he's seen and done. We talk about gods and devils and all the things in between; all of the Dark Ladies. How sometimes even devils bow down before them. Sometimes I let him kiss me.

Other times I don't let him in at all, just wait on the other side of the front door and listen to him breathing, saying my name.

Even angels might make deals with devils in order to do good, when such good cannot be set in motion except by a raging conflagration, just as some seeds will not sprout without the action of a great fire.

Astor Crowley, Queen Priestess of the Society for the Justification of Judas Iscariot, 1982 A.D.

AUTHOR'S NOTE

There is a Wells-next-the-Sea.

There is no St Jude's Isle. The church of St Jude's took some inspiration from a visit to Devon's St Peter's Churchyard at Lewtrenchard, where the great folklorist, Rev. Sabine Baring-Gould is buried.

This novella has a few echoes in it, *The Wicker Man*, *The Red King*, *Rosemary's Baby* perhaps, a little *Hereditary* and a *lot* of the old folk horror movies I saw as a kid, which were already old when I was watching them in the eighties. Plus a little nod to *The League of Gentlemen*.

There are a *lot* of horror novels and novellas involving authors, struggling to create, going somewhere isolated to write, and frequently dragging a variety of sins behind them. Generally it's male authors who come to a bad end. I wanted to make things a bit different. Hence, a female author, who walks a tightrope *between* good and evil, and doesn't fall – yet.

When I first started thinking about this story, Everly popped into my head. I could feel her vibrating against the universe, caught in this weird space between rage and grief and wandering. I wondered how she'd react to finding out that her husband hadn't just been cheating (she sensed that, most women do, somehow) but also that he'd lied about who he was. Maybe it was a lie designed to protect her, back when he loved her, but it simply became another disrespect as time moved on.

I had the name of the firm Higgins & Hyde first and then Albert popped up as their representative. In a year when capitalism has turned even more spectacularly toxic, I thought surely hell is a version of corporate life – there's a long connection between the law and the Devil and those who worship silver and gold. I wanted to poke at the idea of a demon who's been in a job for a really long time and is bored – and I wondered just who or what might interest him and make his life sparkly again. If anyone's wondering, Albert Lowen looks rather a lot like Lee Pace, who would do an excellent job, I'm sure, of playing that part in a film. Just saying.

Angela 'A.G.' Slatter

Brisbane, AUSTRALIA

10 February, 2025

ABOUT THE AUTHOR

ANGELA 'A.G.' SLATTER has won multiple awards and her work has been translated into many languages. She is best known for her Sourdough Universe novels and short stories, including *All the Murmuring Bones*, which was shortlisted for the Queensland Premier's Literary Awards Book of the Year and the Shirley Jackson Award; *The Path of Thorns*, which won both the Aurealis and Australian Shadows Awards; *The Briar Book of the Dead*; and *The Crimson Road*. She has a PhD in Creative Writing, is a graduate of Clarion South and the Tin House Summer Writers Workshop and has judged both the World Fantasy and Aurealis Awards. She lives in Brisbane, Australia, with a superannuated beagle and a TBR pile which will likely be the death of her. Find her on her website angelaslatter.com and on social media @angelaslatter

For more fantastic fiction, author events,
exclusive excerpts, competitions, limited editions and more

VISIT OUR WEBSITE
titanbooks.com

LIKE US ON FACEBOOK
facebook.com/titanbooks

FOLLOW US ON TWITTER AND INSTAGRAM
@TitanBooks

EMAIL US
readerfeedback@titanemail.com